Treaty Brides

THE DESERT BRIDE

SAMANTHA CAYTO

The Desert Bride
ISBN # 978-1-80250-580-1
©Copyright Samantha Cayto 2023
Cover Art by Kelly Martin ©Copyright November 2023
Interior text design by Claire Siemaszkiewicz
Pride Publishing

Published in 2023 by Pride Publishing, United Kingdom.

Collections

THE DESERT BRIDE

Chapter One

Sir Geoffrey Arbuthnott gazed around at the relentlessly barren landscape and sighed. "You know, Lucas, it's times like these that make me truly wish to have been born my parents' third son. The thought of living in a quiet monastery brewing ale has great appeal."

His right-hand man snorted. "No, you don't. Beer-making is only part of your brother's life, and I can't imagine you kneeling on a stone floor in endless prayer. And before you run through your other brotherly options, you would hate farming, politicking and commerce just as much. Being a soldier suits you best, old friend."

Geoffrey watched the king's cartographer, Professor Johns, jump off his wagon seat with surprising alacrity for a man of his age and physique. And he did so while holding a pad of paper and pencil, no less. The man squinted into the distance before sketching furiously.

Geoff suppressed another sigh. "Except this isn't soldiering."

"It could be. Not that it looks like anyone lives in this arid place. I mean, where would they find enough water to drink and to grow food?"

The question highlighted their own predicament. Since entering this desert area far to the west of Moorcondia, he'd implemented strict rationing of their supplies. There was a real possibility that they'd have to turn back soon if they didn't find natural springs to replenish their canteens and flora and fauna to cull for more food. If that happened, it would mean failing, and he'd never done that in his life. Boring this mission may be, but he was determined to make it a success.

"We've seen enough rodents scurrying about, and we'll eat those if nothing else presents itself. The gods know we've dined on worse during our campaigns. There must be sources of water. It's a matter of finding them, that's all." He scanned the skies, and his heart ticked up a beat at the sight of some birds circling in the distance. There." He pointed. "We go in that direction."

Lucas squinted up. "Hmm. Could be promising." He issued a sharp whistle to gain the attention of the other soldiers and waved in the direction they would head.

Once the cartographer had returned to his seat on the wagon, they resumed their journey. They'd traded their warhorses for stout working ones. The beasts weren't made for speed, but they were perfect for plodding along all day. And they'd brought replacements that carried provisions. If worse came to worst, they could always use them as sources of food, although he hated the idea. Previous scouts had warned them of this desert, so they had prepared as best they could. The problem was no one knew how large this area of the world was — and what, if anything other than perhaps ocean, lay on the other side. It was possible it was so vast they'd have to turn around and try again with even more supplies. The idea was depressing. He was a soldier, not an explorer, but with the Marshers subdued and the danger of the Swarm neutralized, his skills were in low demand. A good thing for Moorcondia, but bad thing for someone who'd spent his entire manhood training and fighting.

Geoff kept his gaze on the large birds flying in tight circles up ahead. They were scavengers, he was sure of it, although nothing he'd seen before. The cartographer was a good hand at drawing, as his profession demanded, and the man was memorializing everything he saw. Someone, someday, back in Moorcondia, would give names to every bit of scrub and creature they came across. That part was not his job. He and his men were there to protect Professor Johns. So far, it had been an easy task. The man was eccentric, to be sure, but he was also affable — and seemingly fearless. A recently widowed man, he'd professed a keen desire to make a mark for the remainder of his life, regardless of the risk. One couldn't help but admire the man.

It was hard to judge distance in this environment. What had looked far away proved to be closer. They hadn't gone far before Geoff was delighted to spy some greenery — or at least plants that were less brown than what they'd seen so far. It had to mean a source of water. There was a palpable sense of excitement in his men, although they were too well trained to prod their horses to a greater speed. Conservation of energy was critical, and where there was water, there could be dangerous animals—the human kind, most of all. When they were close enough to make out more detail, Geoff held up his hand to stop the procession.

He signaled two men to go with him, while giving Lucas the order to stay put with the professor and the others. Then he proceeded at the same cautious speed, keeping his eyes fixed on his destination. He took in each detail as they came into focus. It was indeed a large oasis with a wide shimmering pool of water, tall thin trees with leafy greens at the top and…a horse. He stopped and blinked against the glare of the sun to be sure he was seeing correctly. And yes, it was a short, stout dappled horse with only a blanket thrown over its back. It stood to one side of the spot, grazing on some kind of low-lying shrubbery. It didn't appear to be injured or sick, so the scavengers hadn't been drawn by this animal. Not far from it, there was a dark blob seeming to float within the sand just beyond the water. A few steps later, he realized it wasn't bits of carrion as he'd expected, but a head—a human one.

Now he kicked his mount into a fast trot, still scanning the horizon for danger. He slowed again once he'd reached the oasis, skirting the water as he headed for whoever was trapped in the sand. Relief washed over him when the head of hair and the arms attached to the same body moved. Whoever this was, they were alive. As he rounded to the front of the person, his breath caught at the sight of who was in trouble. Geoff hadn't had any discernible expectations of who he'd find, but this vision caught him by surprise, nevertheless. It was a young man, hardly out of boyhood, with coppery skin and long, straight hair, black as night and plaited on both sides. He looked up at him with wide dark-brown eyes.

Reining his horse to a stop, Geoff tried for a reassuring smile. "Don't worry. I'll get you out of there." When the boy didn't respond, he wondered if he'd understood. In his experience, Moorcondians spoke a universal language. Historians believed that all people had sprung from the same place and had spread out as the population grew. Perhaps here, in this uncharted part of the world, a different tongue had developed. No matter… Actions always spoke more eloquently of one's intent. Dismounting, he uncoiled the length of rope tied to his saddle and unfurled it.

"Take hold of this, and I'll pull you out." So saying, he tossed the end toward the boy, careful not to smack him in the face, yet making sure it got within grabbing distance.

The boy didn't take hold of the rope immediately. He kept his gaze on Geoff for a few seconds before slowly taking the end, wrapping it around one small hand and grabbing it with the other. His exhaustion was obvious, leading Geoff to wonder how long he'd been stuck. For sure, the scavengers had sensed an imminent meal. As soon as he was certain the boy had a good grip, Geoff slowly pulled. There was more resistance than he'd expected. They'd run into this sucking sand early in their journey. It was a danger in that it trapped one but was easily dealt with if one had a companion and something to use as leverage to drag the victim out. This particular patch appeared small but held on to the boy with greater tenacity. And with the oblivious horse having neither opposable thumbs nor anything to toss at its master even if it did, this young man had been at great risk.

Why is he alone?

Geoff trusted that his men would be scouting the area for others. Surely there was some kind of civilization nearby and someone would miss this boy eventually. He could only hope that they were inclined to be friendly — or at least grateful for his help in this matter if they came upon them now. None of that was more than a fleeting thought, however. His concentration remained on the boy's gaze, trying to be reassuring with his expression alone, while he carefully pulled him out of the sand. He tried not to pay too much attention to the fact that the boy was exquisite, with slashing cheekbones, long lashes and plump lips. He ignored as well the bare chest, draped by a beaded vest, and the fact that once the boy was fully out of the sand, he wore only a short, tan leather kilt that left his slender legs exposed. His feet were bare.

When the boy was within reach, he held out a hand. With only a brief hesitation, the boy clasped it and let Geoff tug him to a stand on firmer ground. Fine bits of wet sand clung to his otherwise-smooth skin. Geoff had to resist the temptation to wipe it off. His palms fairly itched with the desire to touch. His dick, which had been lethargic during the trip, found new energy. He'd never wanted anyone more in his life than he did this stranger, not that his interest was going anywhere… The last thing the boy needed was to think his savior was only after sex as the price for help.

It didn't matter anyway what Geoff wanted. The boy stood with glazed eyes, panting and swaying. Then he keeled over, right into Geoff's waiting arms.

* * * *

Mica woke to a cool night breeze. Not that he was cold, lying as he was under a light blanket of unfamiliar weave. With a sudden clarity, he remembered what had happened — his stupidly missing the quicksand before he'd sunk too far to escape on his own. He'd been so focused on a flock of birds that he'd forgotten to look where he was going. In one unguarded moment, he'd proven his mother right that he spent too much time with his head in the clouds instead of focusing on where he was headed. The hot sun had taunted him with death, and he'd begun to truly fear he would die before anyone realized he was missing, until a stranger had come to his rescue — a fierce-looking warrior of an unknown people. In the brief moment before he'd fainted, Mica'd had a chance to appreciate the raw, masculine power in front of him.

He could hear the man now, along with others, their deep voices murmuring around him. He kept his eyes closed, afraid of what new predicament he'd found himself in and worried that his people would walk into danger while out looking for him. Then footsteps approached and his heartbeat sped up. He could feel the presence of something big and warm and smelling of leather and horse.

"You're awake, I believe."

Mica forced himself to open his eyes and face whoever this man was. He blinked in surprise more than in an effort to clear his vision. The impact of seeing him again was no less strong this second time around. It was the green eyes he noticed first, his fear replaced by surprise and curiosity. He'd never met anyone with this man's coloring before. His square face was golden and handsome. His hair was light and cropped very close to his head. And he was dressed far too much for the desert, although given the paleness of his skin, that was probably a good barrier from the sun. He was clearly a warrior of his people, yet his expression was kind.

"Have some water," the man said before Mica could form any words.

His thirst was great, as he would have expected, given how long the sun had beaten down on him. When he tried to sit up, however, weakness had him flopping back down. Except the man shot out an arm to cradle Mica's shoulders. He shuddered at the touch, then melted into it, grateful for the strength. The man held a water bag to his mouth, and he drank greedily until he felt slaked. The man seemed to understand that he needed to lie down again, gently lowering him back onto the thin pallet where he lay.

"I thank you," he managed to say, his raspy voice reminding him he'd been trapped in the quicksand for more than a day.

The stranger grinned. "I'm glad to see you awake, finally. This is the first time since you fainted that you've managed to drink voluntarily. We've had to pour the water into you before."

Mica's tired brain had trouble keeping up with the man's strange cadence and syntax, but the words made sense, and he caught up pretty quickly. "It was for how long, my fainting?"

The man scrunched up his face, obviously also getting used to Mica's form of speech. "One night. It's nearly dawn now."

The answer relieved him. It hadn't been more than three days since he'd left home. Some more water, food and rest, and he'd be ready to ride back on his own. "Trouble you for food, may I?"

"Of course." The man gestured to someone else. A man not much older than Mica came trotting up. "Cecil, your patient is awake and asking for food. What do you think would settle best on his stomach?"

The man frowned. "Some broth with a bit of hard tack soaked in it. If he handles that well, we can move on to dried meat."

"Excellent. Go fetch it, please." The older stranger turned his attention back to Mica. Something about his gaze was intimidating—in a good way. "Cecil may be young but he's a well-trained medic." He paused. "I suppose you are curious as to who we are."

Mica nodded, more keen to learn about these strangers now that death was no longer a concern.

The man put his hand on his own chest. "I am Sir Geoffrey Arbuthnott of Moorcondia. Geoff, if you like."

That was a very long name, impressively so. This man was someone of importance, he was sure. Certainly he commanded those around him. Mica gestured toward himself. "Mica, I am." There was nothing more to give about himself, other than a description of the People and where he came from — and that would give away their location. He couldn't take that chance. This man might seem kind now, but he could be here intent on raiding.

The stranger — Geoff — inclined his head. "I'm pleased to meet you, Mica, and let me assure you we mean you no harm. We are explorers for our king and intend merely to travel across this desert to see what is here and beyond. Our journey is about curiosity, not warfare."

Mica let all those words swirl around in his head before replying. "A chief, you have?"

"Yes, although we call him a king."

"The strongest, he is?" It was hard to believe that Geoff wasn't the chief of his people. Mica had never seen a man so big.

Geoff chuckled. "Not exactly. But he does rule us, and he wants to know what this part of the world looks like. I and these others are going to spend a long time traveling. We mean no harm to anyone."

Perhaps it was foolish to take those words at face value. Somehow Mica did. "Believe you, I do."

There was no chance for further talk as Cecil returned with a small wooden bowl. "Ah, many thanks. I'll see to our guest." Geoff took the bowl and turned to Mica. "Do you need help sitting up?"

Mica thought he could manage on his own yet nodded instead. "Please."

Once again, his rescuer wrapped that big, strong arm around his shoulders and lifted him to a sitting position. Mica reveled in the feel of it. No man, other than his father, had ever touched him so, and no one had ever made him feel this funny warmth deep in his belly. His cock tingled with warning. He pressed one hand down on his lap to keep it under control while he tried to take the bowl with the other. Geoff kept hold of it, though, guiding it to his lips. It was caretaking in a way that was both reminiscent of his mother's coddling when he'd been young and also completely different. Perverse as it might be, he was glad to have landed in trouble. If he hadn't, this man might have passed by without a glimpse.

Not that his attraction was going to amount to anything. As he sipped at his broth, he focused on every detail of the experience—the feel of Geoff's strength, the scent of him, the strange sound of his voice and the excitement it incited in his blood. He would make the most of his time with these strangers, and when he returned home, he would keep the knowledge to himself. Unless Geoff was lying about his intent, Mica dared not tell his chief about their lands being trespassed upon. The People had fought hard to claim their place in the world, and warring tribes were always a worry. He knew the chief wouldn't allow Geoff and his men to simply go on their way. The world was a harsh place, and only the strong and ruthless survived.

When he'd had his fill, he lay back down, comfortable but not sleepy. "Of your tribe, tell me you will?"

Geoff sat cross-legged beside him. "Certainly. Will you also tell me about yours?"

Mica lowered his eyes, disappointed. "Cannot."

There were a few moments of silence. "Ah well, fair enough. I don't want you to get in trouble or worry about my intent. I am happy to tell you about my country, though."

It was like being a child again, lying on his pallet, listening to a fun tale. Geoff talked about great stone dwellings that stood on their own, surrounded by lush trees and shrubbery with many flowers. People rode horses but also in large carts, and they clothed themselves in many layers. It was cold in his country during one season with something called 'snow' that seemed too fantastical to be real. Geoff explained more about what they were doing and the role of the older man who was more the size of Mica's people with a pot belly and hair only on the sides of his head. This man was making drawings of everything he saw to take back one day to show their king. It was an amazing story and one that lulled him back to sleep before he was ready.

Still, he wasn't afraid. Against all reason, he was sure he was safe with Sir Geoffrey Arbuthnott—a strange man with a long name and the kindness to save the life of someone and ask nothing in return.

* * * *

Mica patted the side of Windmaker's neck, happy to see that she'd been cared for as much as he had. The sun had climbed well into the sky. He had recovered from his ordeal and his provisions were just as he'd left them in his pack, now strapped across his back. His knife was once more belted across his waist. Geoff and his men had taken nothing from him, even as they'd given him back his life. All those warnings from the elders about the danger of others had proven to be untrue with respect to these Moorcondians. It gave him hope that someday the People would not live in isolation. That day had not yet come, however, and he needed to warn Geoff to stay well away from the warriors that roamed the perimeter of the Peoples' land.

He turned to look for Geoff to bid him a reluctant farewell and was surprised to find the man already upon him. He and his men were packed to also leave the oasis.

"Do you have everything you need, Mica?"

Suddenly shy now that he wasn't an invalid, Mica dropped his gaze. "Yes."

"Good. Thanks to this oasis, we do as well. I hope there are more along the way."

Mica nodded. "Find them, you will."

"I'm glad to hear it. Ah," Geoff stepped closer. "I have enjoyed our time together, even though it was based on your difficulties."

Mica lifted his gaze. "Like it as well, I did."

The man's gaze changed. It took on an intense, heated look. "Will you permit me to say good-bye in the way of my people when we part from someone...whose company we like?"

With the man's gaze now focused on Mica's lips, he thought he knew what was coming. The thought of it thrilled him and closed up his throat. He could only nod.

Geoff moved slowly, lowering his mouth to Mica's. There was plenty of time to evade the kiss. That was the last thing he wanted, however, and when they touched, he closed his eyes and had to bite back a moan. It was over far too quickly. When Geoff pulled away, Mica had to resist the urge to lunge at him.

Geoff chuckled. "That was unkind of me, to us both. It was like giving a thirsty man only a drop of water. I wish we had more time, Mica."

He took in a deep breath, savoring his name on the man's tongue. Then he forced his eyes open and himself to accept reality. This was a brief encounter, nothing more. He would live with the memory and already knew that no man could ever match his desire for Geoff.

Grabbing Windmaker's mane, he vaulted onto her back. There was one last thing he could do for this man who would never be anything more than his fantasy lover. Pointing toward the Peoples' village, he said, "That way, you do not go. Understand?" He peered at the man, willing him to do so without further explanation. It was a risk, but one he felt confident in taking.

Geoff stared at a distance with a stern expression. Then, he smiled at Mica. "Yes, I will heed your warning. I don't want trouble for anyone—you, least of all." He stepped back. "Safe travels, Mica. And stay away from quicksand."

Mica allowed himself one last, long look at the man who'd saved his life while leaving him wanting, before kicking his horse to a gallop. The sooner he returned home, the sooner he could find somewhere private to relive his fantasy.

Chapter Two

Mica saw the group of warriors when he was nearly home. With the sun beginning her descent to rejoin the Earth Mother for the night, he'd hoped he would make it back on his own. The sight of these men coming to look for him caused him to spur Windmaker to greater speed. Although he'd put a lot of distance between himself and the strangers, he wanted to be sure to give the warriors no reason to venture farther than this. The chief would have been the one to order them out as a search party for him, but his mother would have prodded the man into action. Of that, he was sure. He'd been gone too long for her not to worry, and as the shaman of the People as well as the chief's sister, she had great sway with him and usually got her way.

Mica felt guilty about causing any problems and forcing others to waste their time. Not that he'd planned on getting into trouble, but it was still his fault. He'd already concocted a story of his losing track of time and chasing after a strange bird. It was believable, given his wandering ways and the general perception that he was prone to daydreaming. And it was far better than admitting he'd been distracted and stupid enough to step into quicksand. No one of the People should ever be so careless, let alone someone ready for his manhood initiation. There was a tongue-lashing in his near future, and it was no more than he deserved. But he wasn't going to repay the kindness of the man called Geoff by sending warriors after him.

His heart sank a bit when he was close enough to see who led the men. *Lonan*. The warrior was always currying favor with Mica's family, trying to advance himself within the warrior rank and get closer to the chief. He was the only son of tanners, an important way to serve the People, yet without high status. Lonan was known to be ambitious, had developed admirable skills as a warrior and had a reputation for being fearless — if not vicious to their enemies. There had been talk lately of his marrying Mica's sister. The idea bothered Mica, given how the man always seemed more interested in him than Alyn. Although he was inexperienced in sex, there was no misunderstanding the lust in Lonan's gaze. And while Mica yearned for the chance to be bedded by a man, Lonan's interest in him made his skin crawl. There was something...predatory about his attention.

The moment that the warriors pulled up their horses in front of him, Lonan raked Mica up and down with his gaze. "In one piece you are, I see." Lonan gave a mean-looking smile. "Pleased the shaman will be that into carrion, her oldest son hasn't turned."

Mica schooled his own expression to one of indifference. He instinctively knew he shouldn't show weakness in front of this man. "Quite well I am, and apology I owe my mother. Sorry I must say for your

Samantha Cayto

wasted journey." He kicked Windmaker to keep walking.

Lonan shot his hand out and grabbed Mica as he passed, forcing him to stop. "Your childish ways you must end, Mica. Ready for your manhood initiation, one might believe you are not. Perhaps for another passing of the seasons, a boy you should remain."

Mica reined in his temper, even as he did the same with Windmaker. Being a smart beast, she didn't like Lonan's proximity. It made her ears twitch, and she stomped and snorted in an effort to move away. Mica held her in place and lifted his chin. "For the chief and shaman that is to decide." *And want that you don't, anyway, because on your pallet you may not have me if a child I remain.* He knew enough to guard his tongue. As a warrior, Lonan was entitled to respect, especially when there were a half-dozen other men around to hear. Mica didn't want to do anything worthy of punishment. There was no winning any battle he might fight with the man, anyway. He did stare him down, however, silently challenging the warrior to keep him from leaving. As childish as Mica might be perceived, he was the shaman's son and the chief's nephew. That gave him a higher status than any of the warriors that were here with him.

Lonan was no fool. Still, he shot Mica a smirk before letting go. Mica kicked Windmaker into a trot and paid the warriors no mind as they surrounded him on the way back home. Although ostensibly they were there to protect him, he couldn't shake the feeling that he was imprisoned by them—that if he tried to break free, they'd chase him down and return him to the place they believed he belonged. And the growing problem for Mica was that he increasingly felt as if he didn't. Each

23

time he dared take some time for himself, he wandered farther away, looking for nothing in particular, merely knowing there was *more* out there and wanting to see it for himself. Rambling and some amount of aimlessness was fine for children, encouraged even. Once he'd passed into manhood, he would be forced to settle into his responsibility to the People. There would be no more wandering for him, and the thought of it saddened him.

As they walked through the widening canyon that led to the village, Mica couldn't help but see the high sandstone walls as a kind of trap. There were only two ways in and out, a configuration that made it both easier to defend from marauding tribes and gave them a path for escaping if the worst were to happen. He knew, though, that it also meant there was no easy way for any of the People to leave the tribe for good. Anyone who tried would be seen and brought back, much as was being done with him now. Every one of them existed for the greater good, and while part of him was ashamed to long for the freedom to leave, he wanted to…more so now that he knew for sure there were people other than desert tribes in the world. If Geoff were to be believed, there existed many different places and people—exotic and fascinating ones—to explore and meet. His life among the People had never felt so small to him as he entered the village proper, hemmed in by the warriors, the high canyon cliffs and a narrow way of life that he'd been born into.

Dwelling on any of that was unhelpful, however. He could do so later that night as he lay alone on his pallet…assuming he was interested in torturing himself again with what was and what couldn't be. With his family sleeping nearby, he wouldn't be able to pleasure himself while reliving his time with the desirable stranger, the very thought of whom caused his heartbeat to quicken and his dick to harden. Good thing the thong he wore under his kilt for modesty kept it under control. Normally he used his time alone outside the village to indulge in such activities, but with his latest escapade, there would be no chance of leaving any time soon. And there was no quiet sneaking back in as he'd hoped. The procession he and the warriors made as they rode through the center of the village caused everyone to stop and stare as they went by.

Mica kept his gaze averted, yet felt his cheeks heat at the scrutiny. He had no one to blame other than himself. If he'd been more careful… No, it was hard to regret what had happened, given that his mistake had led to him meeting the enthralling Geoff and his fascinating band of warriors. It wasn't merely how attracted he was to the man. The idea that they could all simply leave their homes to spend many seasons exploring what was beyond their known world was equally enticing. Knowing that they existed and what they were doing was probably the most exciting thing that would ever happen to him. The experience would stay with him for the rest of his life and get him through what he expected to be lonely nights.

His mother was already lining up suitable women for him to marry. He knew he could never bring himself to do so. If he were patient, he could move into a small dwelling of his own near the stables. He would miss living with others, but it would be better than spending the rest of his life lying next to someone whom he couldn't want. If the Earth Mother had made men for women, she'd missed the mark with him.

At the stables, Lonan and the other men broke off to put up their horses, as Mica did the same. The horse master ignored the others and came over to greet him.

"Mica, worried you had us all." The kindly old man, who was his mentor, slipped a rope around Windmaker's neck and stood by her head while Mica dismounted.

"Apologies, Master Noshi. Work extra I will, to make up for the lost time."

Noshi shook his head. "Necessary that is not. Already harder you work than most men and deserve it you do to savor the last of your childhood. Too many of the People there are invested in pushing you into manhood as quickly as possible." His gaze slid over to Lonan. "When return you didn't in your usual time, ready was your mother to send out a rescue party. Yesterday, demand it she did. Insisted your father to wait to see if back you came on your own. Old enough to take care of yourself you are, even though not yet your manhood ceremony has happened. Waiting, the shaman liked not, but had his way your father did — for once. Glad I am to see right he was, that in any trouble you were not. Good was your final wandering I hope."

Mica called up a smile. "Good it was, Master Noshi." That was no lie. Other than the part where he'd been stuck in the quicksand and worried he might die, it had been a good time. And any doubt Mica had had about keeping secret the full extent of his adventure disintegrated. The last thing he wanted was to get into the middle of a disagreement between his parents and prove his mother right in the matter. As shaman, she was second only to the chief, which had an extra layer of complexity, given that he was her brother. That wasn't always the case. It had just so happened that the

Earth Mother had called to her as a matter of birthright, and her brother had grown into the biggest and best warrior of his generation. Being her husband was a place of great status for his father, but as a proud warrior, the man had difficulty ceding authority to her within the family. The man didn't need confirmation that his wife had been right about something that should be in the purview of a warrior.

He took the rope from Noshi. "Wrong of me it was to lose track of time as I did, though. My mother would be worried, I should have known. Possible it is not my manhood ceremony to put off. Waited I have longer than most. Want it now, I do."

He wasn't being entirely truthful. He'd been of two minds about crossing into adulthood officially. A man, even one who wasn't a warrior, didn't have to answer to his parents anymore. He'd have the right to do as he pleased within the confines of his duties to the People and the rules set down by the chief. Mica craved that type of freedom, but with it came the responsibility of running the stable with Noshi. He had to be ready to take over as the master of the horses when the time came. It was a good choice of work for him. He had no real aptitude for fighting, and his slight frame meant he would always be at a disadvantage in warfare. He had no skill at crafting, either. Tending to the horses came naturally to him. He really had no reason to complain and yet…the more important his role within the tribe became, the more certain it would be that he could never leave, never do anything to change his fate. That foolish hope, however unlikely to happen, wasn't simply dying. It was already dead.

"See to the warriors' mounts, I will do, sir. Then the shaman's forgiveness I will beg."

It didn't take long to rub down the horses and place them in the corral. Still, the sun was disappearing on the horizon by the time he'd finished. There was no longer a reason to linger at the stables. He couldn't put off any longer his return to the family dwelling to face his mother. He washed up at the stable in order to be reasonably presentable and slipped on the clean moccasins he kept there. Because of his mother's high status, his home was in the middle of the settlement. Walking from the stables at the far end meant he had to pass even more people on his way. There were some smiles and hands raised in greeting. Others gave him a knowing look, ready for the shaman's heated greeting to ring out over the village. Her voice tended to carry, so there were no secrets about what happened in their family.

He raced up the steps carved into the mountain to the first level of dwellings. The moment he stepped into his family's cave, he smelled dinner. His sister was tending to the pot of stew while also frying up flatbread on the hot stone beside it. She shook her head at him as he passed, but he barely noticed. It was the figure sitting at the loom at the far end of the main room that held his attention. He approached his mother with a hanging head and waited patiently for her to acknowledge him once he arrived.

Atrina was scrutinizing her latest weave, looking for flaws, no doubt—and finding none, he was sure. The shaman didn't make mistakes, not in her crafts, her pronouncements of the People's law or most importantly, the will of the Earth Mother. She knew how to wield her power, too, and making someone wait was a common method of asserting her dominance.

Her silent disapproval was almost as bad as her biting words would be.

Finally, she looked up. "To wait one more day before sending out a search party your father wanted. Correct in this matter was he, and wrong I was, given finding you so close to home the warriors did." Her quiet, flat tone surprised him and also confirmed that she was more irked about his father being right and not her than she was about his staying away so long.

Mica winced. "Sorry I am, Mother, for causing you worry. Caught up in following a new species of bird on our land I became. Lost track of time," he confessed and hung his head even lower.

His mother pursed her lips. "Hmm. Too much time with your gaze upon the clouds instead of on your feet you spend. Ground you, your initiation into manhood will. Hope we all do, anyway," she muttered. Then in a louder voice, "Unable to accomplish it your father and I have been. My prayers often the Earth Mother has heard. A wife and family you need. Help you settle they will."

Mica knew better than to say anything. He really did and should have been grateful he was getting off so easily. His thoughts burst out anyway. "Marry must I?" He clamped his lips shut, instantly regretting his outburst, especially as he knew the answer already.

His mother narrowed her gaze. "A ridiculous question that is. Must you, of course. Everyone does, and in waiting there is no point. Do so first your sister will, naturally. Soon after your manhood initiation celebration her marriage will be, I think. Until after the harvest for your wedding we will wait. Yes," she added with a nod, speaking more to herself than him. "The most sense that timing makes."

"Marrying Lonan I will not," his sister called out.

Their mother's eyes flashed with anger as she stood from her loom. At least she was no longer focused on Mica. "A perfectly fine choice Lonan is, Alyn. A fierce warrior he is, and as the future shaman, someone strong by your side you will need. His humble status matters not."

Mica wished she felt the same way about his future prospects, that he also needed someone strong and protective. The idea of a warrior like Geoff taking care of him was thrilling. He knew he wasn't supposed to have these feelings, yet he couldn't help it. Ever since he'd been young, he'd been drawn to men, not women. Warriors found pleasure with other men before marriage. He'd seen hints of that himself, and it wasn't exactly a secret. But physical release was one thing. A lifelong commitment to each other was another. There was no hope for what he wanted. His best outcome for the future was to avoid marrying anyone. It would take a great deal of effort to defy his mother on this point. If Alyn put off her own marriage, it would at least buy him time.

Alyn put the last of the flat bread she was making on a plate already containing a mound of thick stew and stood away from the cooking fire. "Like him I do not. Too obvious his efforts are to gain status through marrying me. Respectful to you he seems. Dismissive of me I find. Like Father, he is not." She shook her head. "Find someone else I will."

Their mother put her hands on her hips. "If to pick that potter you mean…"

"A fine man Yancy is. And beautiful crockery he makes. As you say about Lonan, status matters not."

"And protect you how with those pots would he? Over an attacker's head he would break them?"

"If failed to repel our enemies our warriors have, to the extent into our dwellings they enter, our last line of defense pots and plates may actually be." She threw up her hands. "My mind I have not yet made up, Mother. Pressured into accepting Lonan I will not be. In any event, ready our supper is."

"Perfect my timing is, I see." Their father entered with Mica's little brother in his arms, his large frame filling the space.

If Chief Chayton hadn't been that much bigger and stronger, Keme might have been chief. It was rare for the shaman and the chief to be wedded, but it also made for an easier marriage, he'd heard. With more equal status came necessary harmony. Mica both admired his father and feared him — or rather feared disappointing him. He knew he wasn't the kind of son the man had expected to have.

Lye, Mica's little brother, was a second chance for the man. It had been a great sorrow in their family that their mother had lost three babies after Mica. Lye had come out of their mother's womb with a hearty wail and a vigorous sucking at her breast. He was a chubby toddler now and a late-in-life gift from the Earth Mother. The boy's feet rarely touched the ground, their father carrying him around with him nearly all day, as if letting him out of sight would mean losing him. That obvious worry was the most weakness he'd ever seen in the man, and no one blamed him for it, not even their mother.

When their father approached, Lye squealed and held his arms out to Mica. He took the child into his own embrace without question. He adored his baby brother and hoped that he would truly grow into the kind of man their father wanted in a son. The Earth Mother knew Mica was never going to be that, even if his father had never said as much.

As their father handed Lye over, he eyed Mica. "In one piece you are, I see. In your wanderings, any trouble there was?"

"No, sir." Mica focused on his brother, hating that he wasn't telling the truth. That wasn't like him, and it wasn't merely an effort to save his own hide from the wrath and ridicule the truth would bring. Protecting Geoff from discovery by the People and the almost certain harm that would come from it had taken root deep inside him. His lie served both purposes.

His father nodded. "Then no more about it shall we speak. Eat now, let us."

They sat cross-legged around the stone table covered with one of his mother's blankets. Mica set Lye on his lap and helped the boy with his food. It was good to be home, and his ordeal out in the desert had left him tired. As he settled into the rhythm of everyday life, it was almost as if his perilous experience in the quicksand followed by his amazing rescue had never happened. Mica pushed visions of Geoff and the reaction of his body from just thinking about the man to the back corner of his mind. He concentrated on listening to the usual chatter of his family that came at the end of the day as he helped himself to the warm comfort of his sister's meal.

"Spoken to the chief I have," his father said. "In two suns' time, take place your manhood initiation shall."

It took Mica a moment to realize his father was talking to him. Handing over a bite of stew wrapped in flat bread to Lye, Mica looked at the man. "So soon?"

He winced inwardly. That hadn't been what he'd meant to say. That wasn't how any child was expected to respond when finding out they were finally going to cross into adulthood.

He was supposed to be excited to be tested into manhood. And he mostly was — sort of. He was also a bit frightened. It wasn't going to be easy. That was the whole point. And it was nothing like his explorations out in the desert. Little of the skills he'd learned doing that would help with what was coming — or so he assumed. For boys, the event was shrouded in mystery. All he knew was that it happened inside the mountain that shaded them, but they didn't enter for any other reason. He much preferred the initiation for girls into womanhood. There were no hidden frights with it. All they had to do was show prowess in dressing and butchering game, grinding grain finely to make soft flatbread and running the outside perimeter of the village to show that they had stamina and could always find their way home. Mica figured he would be better at those kinds of tests than the one he was facing.

His father frowned, his gaze making Mica want to squirm. The man was a mighty warrior, blooded from defending the People. In his own way, he was as intimidating as Mica's mother, even though he didn't hold as high a status. "Past time it is. Why questioning it you are? Unsure of your readiness you are?"

Mica knew there was only one acceptable answer. Keme had undoubtedly faced his own ceremony with ease. Knowing the man as he did, it was impossible to think otherwise, even though no man spoke of what happened to him during his own test of manhood. Only a man's warrior guide knew, and it was understood to be a guarded secret. "No, sir. Ready I am."

His father grunted. "Hope so, I should. To spend so much time in the desert as anyone can on his own, the test into manhood he should pass."

"Yes, sir." Mica said nothing more. The decision had been made, and honestly, he was somewhat surprised the matter had been raised with him prior to the day of the initiation. Of anyone in the family, Mica had the least say of what happened. Even his siblings held more sway. He wasn't going to be a shaman like Alyn or a warrior, which the sturdy Lye was clearly going to grow into. He was destined to tend to the horses, an important role for the People, to be sure. But no one thought of him as having any power whatsoever. Normally he wouldn't care, knowing nothing else. Now, he chafed at his situation and had to hide his resentment. Since his encounter with the faraway stranger, however, he really wished he had control over his own destiny.

* * * *

"Stop! Stop!"

Geoff pulled his horse around and held up his hand to his men. The cartographer was already hopping off his wagon, his spyglass in his hand.

"What is it, Professor?" He rode back to the man and tamped down his impatience as the man raised the glass to his eye and peered at a distant canyon. This was the whole purpose of their journey, after all — exploration. It didn't matter that the sun was setting and that they needed to make camp soon.

The small man lowered his glass and pointed excitedly toward where he'd been looking. "I think I see signs of civilization over there. I think there are crops growing on the tops of the canyon walls. Perhaps that's where the boy came from."

Geoff didn't have to look to know the answer to that speculation. He'd led his expedition along their original path, perpendicular to the direction Mica had ridden, without explanation. He'd hoped no one would question the move, given that it wasn't a deviation from the westward trajectory of their journey. But Johns' keen eyes missed nothing, and it was now clear that the desert wasn't laid out in neat lines, that they'd come upon what was perhaps the back of the place the boy had come from. The canyon in the distance had a curve to it. If they went through it, he expected they would end up north of the oasis, essentially back to where they'd come from.

With Mica's warning ringing in his ears, he tried to dissuade the cartographer from his curiosity. As a soldier, Geoff wasn't shy about engaging with any danger. But they were there to explore, not conquer. Avoiding a confrontation was important. Plus, however much he yearned to see the boy again, he didn't want their meeting to end in bloodshed. No one would be happy about that, least of all Mica, should Geoff kill any of his people. And the outcome of a fight wasn't certain. Dispatching the occasional brigand was one thing. Facing off a whole village of armed men was another.

"Professor, you may be right, but where there is civilization, there is the danger of confrontation. We are not on a diplomatic mission. Avoiding other people will make our job of exploration of the land easier."

The man practically jumped up and down in his objection. "No, no, Sir Geoffrey. Mapping the location of other people is just as important as the landscape.

The king needs to know what to find when he sends others this way. And I'm not suggesting we approach them, merely catalog their existence. Aren't you curious as to whether it's possible to cultivate any crops in this environment?"

Not really. That was churlish of him. What did he know about exploration, other than how to wield a sword in protection of those who did? He wasn't there to second-guess the professor, either. If he hadn't stumbled upon Mica, would he really object to satisfying the cartographer's curiosity quite so strongly?

No.

Resigned to doing what was needed of him, he nodded. "You're right, sir. We will head in that direction...tomorrow morning." When the man opened his mouth with an obvious objection, Geoff overrode him. "The sun is getting low. How much can you see in the dark? We make camp here." He lifted his voice to encompass everyone. "We'll break camp at dawn and make our way to the canyon. But," he added with a stern look, "we will not go too far in. If there are people living within it, they will not welcome what could appear to be marauders. My orders are to avoid confrontation whenever possible. Is that understood, sir?" he added with a stern look at the professor.

Johns grimaced before shooting him a surprising grin. "Very well. My wife always did say that my curiosity would be the death of me. I don't intend to prove her right on this journey." With that, the man wandered back to the wagon to pull out his sketch pad.

Relieved that the man's amenability proved stronger than his stubbornness, Geoff dismounted and let a soldier take his horse to tend for him. He stood with his hands on his hips and his gaze on the fuzzy distance. Somewhere out there was Mica. He couldn't help wondering how the boy was. Had he made it back home all right? Did Mica think of him as much as he'd been thinking of Mica? It was ridiculous how much thoughts of the boy had intruded during the day's ride. It took no effort to envision Mica's surprisingly smooth skin and the silky feel of his black hair. The mere thought of those doe-brown eyes staring at him made him hard and needy. Such a young, likely innocent boy shouldn't affect him so. He'd always been attracted to hardened soldiers such as himself. The occasional tumble with a lithesome whorehouse lad had left him wanting. If he wanted to be delicate with his lovers, he would seek out women. The desert stranger should have held no more interest for him. Yet he did, distractingly so.

He'd been without a bed companion for too long, that was all — and his own damn fault. Later that night, as all but the first-watch soldiers bedded down, the men would pair off for a bit of pleasure before sleep. Any one of his men would gladly suck his cock or offer up his ass to him — if that's what he wanted. There was no shame in giving release to a man of higher status, and he was well-liked among those he'd picked for this journey. Lucas had said as much, even if Geoff hadn't been sure of his men's views of him and was, himself, always willing to give Geoff relief. It would take no more than a raised eyebrow to get some pleasure that night. But even with his balls aching and his cock straining, Geoff had been tamping down his own needs since the journey had begun and knew he wasn't going to take anyone up on their willingness to change that for him. It wouldn't be enough, because it wouldn't be Mica.

And that was a crying shame. His journey had become that much harder.

* * * *

Professor Johns eagerly offered his spyglass to Geoff. "Take a look for yourself. I was right. Those are crops far off on the top of both sides of the canyon, and if I'm not mistaken, there are recesses carved into the walls themselves. People have made homes out of the cliffs and have figured out a way to cultivate food, even in this dry environment. There is more to this area than we've seen so far. It is most exciting."

Geoff dutifully did as the man asked, although he was sure of the rightness of his deductions. This had to be where Mica had come from, which meant there was possible danger waiting farther inside the canyon. They were already hemmed in, having traveled past the opening more than he'd wanted. Johns had been most insistent that he needed a better look to sketch this part of the desert accurately. But it was time for Geoff to take back control and assert his power as the military leader of the expedition. He wasn't going to take the risk of an attack, especially as any more detail would be useless to them. They weren't going to linger in this desert long enough to cultivate their own food. The details of how this was being done might be interesting, but not necessary for the mission.

He folded the spyglass and handed it back to the cartographer. "Yes, I can see that you're right, and of course, you must catalog all of this for future exploration. For now, we turn around and head once again westward."

Johns screwed up his face with displeasure. "You are interfering with the mission. You're supposed to be helping me explore."

Geoff leaned over his saddle to get closer to the man. "Yes, and my duty also includes keeping your skin intact. My military acumen is warning me that this is a dangerous place, and that, sir, overrides your opinion. We're leaving." Geoff signaled his men with a wave of his arms.

Just as everyone, including the wagon, was facing the end of the canyon, an arrow landed right in front of the point man. Geoff reined in his horse and whipped out his sword at the same time. All his men did so, and every pair of eyes was cast upward. *Fuck.* High on top of either side of the walls stood men, stretched out along the ridge line to cover Geoff's men from front to back. And each soldier had a notched arrow pointed down at them. Geoff turned his horse in a circle to take it all in. They were trapped. Even at a full gallop, many of them would be struck down, and that said nothing of the problem of getting the wagon and Professor Johns out. Geoff mentally kicked himself. He should have been firmer with the cartographer and put safety above the mission to explore as much as they could.

The situation had to be defused if they stood any chance of leaving alive. "Put your swords away!" To a man, his soldiers complied with the order, testament to their training overriding their instinct to fight.

As he contemplated his next move, the sounds of galloping horses reached them. Seconds later, a group of about a dozen men came riding around a bend in the canyon. They were dressed as Mica had been and as those archers on the top of the walls were, with bare chests, beaded vests and short swords — or rather, long knives — belted around their kilts. Unlike Mica, they wore soft boots up to their knees, but also like the boy, had no tack on their horses. Most of them had arrows at the ready and controlled their mounts with their legs alone. It was an impressive feat that he would have admired if his men's lives weren't at risk.

The leader of those who approached had his hand on the hilt of his weapon, only with no bow or quiver slung over his back. He stopped out of reach of any of Geoff's soldiers. He was younger than Geoff and of an age of most of the others, and he was no less fit and formidable-looking. The man looked down his slightly hooked nose. "In charge, who is?"

Geoff didn't hesitate to walk his horse forward to face the man. "I am."

Chapter Three

Geoff held the desert warrior's gaze, trying not to show any aggression or disrespect, while at the same time, not cowering in fear. His mind churned with ideas of how to extricate his men from the situation without loss of blood. There was no doubt that they were at a disadvantage with the archers on either side of them ready to rain arrows into the canyon. It was entirely likely that this exploration would end in all of them dying, with no one in Moorcondia even knowing they'd gone missing for years to come. Their fate would almost certainly never be known, and despite that outcome being an accepted risk when they'd volunteered, he still didn't want their journey to end that way.

The warrior scowled. "The People's land you invade."

His time with Mica, however brief, made it easy for him to understand this man's syntax. The words were all the same. It was merely a different ordering of verbs and nouns. He considered trying to mimic it, then decided it might come off as condescending. "My apologies, but invasion was not our intent. We are merely on a journey of exploration to see what lies beyond the border of our country. Our intent is peaceful."

The expression on the warrior's face made it clear he was working to understand Geoff's manner of speech and also didn't believe what he was saying for a second. His words confirmed it. "Lying you are. Raiding your intention is."

Ignoring the ratcheting in tension he could sense on both sides, Geoff pulled out all his diplomatic skills, such as they were. "No, sir, it is not. We will leave here immediately, and you won't see us again. You have my word on that."

Geoff's heart sank as he could see that his reassurances fell on deaf ears. This fairly young man probably thought only in terms of warfare. He might be in the 'kill now, ask questions later' mindset of those not given to the complicated thinking of people higher up the decision chain. If Geoff could get to speak with the chief of this tribe, he'd have a better chance to save the lives of his party.

"Will you take me to your chief so that I may explain myself to him? I'll come with you — unarmed, of course," he hastily added. "And my men will make camp here until I return." *If I return.* No, he couldn't think like that.

There was a long silence, with only the stomping of horse's hooves and wordless whispers of unease from all the men present. The lead warrior kept staring at him as he no doubt contemplated what the best course of action was. Perhaps no one else had ever made such a request. It was entirely possible that the tribes living in this seemingly vast desert area had only ever known warfare. Trading and diplomacy might be an unfamiliar concept to them.

Finally the man responded. He nodded his head once, firmly, and hardened his already stern expression. "Come you may. Here your warriors stay. Unarmed all of you shall be."

Damn, that wouldn't do. Even though he really wasn't in a position to bargain, Geoff had no choice but to try. Besides, he figured a soldier would appreciate strength. "That I cannot agree to. I will strip myself of all weaponry and put myself under your guard, but while my men remain here, they must also be fully armed." He glanced up deliberately at the warriors on the cliffs. "You'll continue to have them at a disadvantage, naturally."

That obvious truth seemed to do the trick. When the man nodded once, Geoff turned his horse around and went back to Lucas. "Here... Take my sword and dagger." He unbuckled his belt with slow movements so as not to appear to be launching an aggression to the indigenous warriors and handed it over.

Lucas took the offering with obvious unhappiness. "This is a terrible idea, sir."

"Do you have a better one? How long do you think we could last if we try to run with arrows loosed upon us?" He considered keeping the knife shoved into his boot, then decided that if he kept any weaponry, he was courting trouble. He held it out, hilt first. "And this."

Lucas grimaced as he accepted it. "You are going into this like a lamb to slaughter."

"I am aware, but there is no hope for it. Does that guy strike as the thinking type?"

Lucas narrowed his gaze past Geoff. "Hmm. No, not really. He strikes me as a hot-headed man itching to let some blood. I'm surprised, frankly, that he's agreed to take you to his chief while we twiddle our thumbs here."

"As am I. There is no reason for him to pretend to do so, then attack the rest of you. Be ready just in case, though. And, Lucas, no matter what happens to me, you must do what is best for the rest of the men. Avenging me is not permitted. Do you understand?"

Lucas' expression conveyed how unhappy that order made him. He nodded, nevertheless. "Yes, sir."

"Good. Sacrificing everyone in vain is not what I want for all of you, and I can't go to my fate, whatever that might be with the worry. You will *not* be the aggressor, no matter what, and if they attack, you fight as best you can, of course—not that there's much hope for escape. And there will be no chance to protect Professor Johns. If it comes down to a few of our men getting away while he and others don't, do so. No sense in everyone dying."

"And yet, I fear we will." Lucas flashed a grin before adding, "Good luck to us all, sir."

Geoff gave a curt nod before scouring the rest of his compliment with a look of more confidence than he felt. Not a man showed any fear, but they did give him looks of respect. As he turned his horse around, once more, Johns surprised him by hopping off his wagon. His abrupt movement sent a wave of new alertness through all of them—Moorcondians and indigenous warriors alike.

"What are you doing, Professor?"

The small man looked up at him. "Your going with these people makes no sense. As a representative of the king, I should be the one to explain our mission. I may not be a diplomat per se, but educating people is part of my old profession. I know how to be persuasive, Sir Geoffrey."

The man had balls, he'd give him that. As patiently as he knew how and mindful of the growing restlessness of their attackers, Geoff explained the hard truths. "Thank you for your offer, sir, but it's not some courtier I go to see. These people are undoubtedly ruled by someone who fights and doesn't simply sit on a throne while others do so for him." Mica's question about whether the king was the strongest of them rang in his memory. "He will be a warrior, sir, who will need to be spoken to as one. Please remain here with Lucas and do as he says."

Johns was clearly unhappy with that answer. "Very well. Good luck to you, Sir Geoffrey. And I look forward to hearing what you say about how these people live. I imagine it's fascinating."

Geoff could only shake his head internally at the man's single-minded focus. He wasn't sure he'd have any opportunity to say anything to anyone ever again. He was getting ahead of himself, though. He returned to the warrior in charge and made no objection to their tying his hands in front of him and taking his reins to lead his horse. As he left the relative comfort of his men, he couldn't help wondering if he'd see Mica again. It was an odd thing to think about, given the dire circumstances of both him and his men. Still, he couldn't help thinking that if he caught a glimpse of the boy, it might make his fate more bearable.

* * * *

Despite his obvious peril, Geoff found himself acting not unlike Professor Johns as he was led through the local village. As the man had surmised, these people had indeed carved their lives out of the canyon walls — literally. At the point in which the canyon widened, a mountain range rose, serving as a backdrop to the life established at its base. There was a bustle of life here not unlike one might find in Moorcondia. He passed a stable, and stalls lined the way on both sides containing various household items such as pottery, woven cloth, metal and tanned leather. Various types of livestock were penned here and there with newly slaughtered animals hanging to dry in the relentless sun.

Higher up, however, was where the difference between the two cultures was to be found. Just as Johns had said, dwellings resided inside the rock past rounded open doorways that showed blackness within. The carved recesses existed on multiple levels that ran the length of the village and obviously were forged by these people as well. Stairs were set in various places to give access to each open floor. At the top, on the flat surface at the base of the mountain that traveled down the canyon, he caught glimpses of low-lying crops. Small figures could be seen walking among them — tending to them, no doubt.

As much as Geoff was taking in his destination, the people along the way didn't hide their curiosity about him. Everyone stopped whatever they'd been doing to watch him being led to whatever his fate was going to be. There were women and girls interspersed with more warriors as were male craftsmen. They were clothed slightly more modestly, the women in dresses made out of soft brown leather and the men in loose shirts over kilts. Colorful beads were woven into both clothing and hair of both sexes. Everyone looked well-fed, and while they all gave the warriors on horseback a wide berth, no one showed any particular fear of them.

Geoff assumed that his journey was heading to the chief of these people as he'd been asked and could only hope that the man had both intelligence and compassion. This was his one chance to save his men, and if the price for doing so was his own sacrifice…? Well, that was the role of a leader after all. He tamped down the fear threatening to swamp him just as he'd learned to do in battle. He was a soldier, still and always. Facing death was his duty.

At a spot he measured to be about mid-point of the settlement, his destination came into view. A round dais had been carved out of more stone. On it stood a man Geoff judged to be about his father's age. He was larger all around than the warriors Geoff had seen so far, with a lined face and a slight paunch that was overtaken by the thickly layered muscle of his chest and arms. The man was dressed like all the other men, except he wore on his head a stiff, round hat woven with red beads. Beside him stood a woman of similar age. She wore no hat, but her hair was intricately braided with the same red beads. Whoever she was, her status was clearly equal to the chief, given her location. They both wore scowls on their faces as they tracked his approach.

Not a warm welcome, then. Hardly surprising.

Geoff let himself be pulled off his horse when they stopped a few feet from the dais. He made sure to stand straight, sensing that size did matter to these people. And while he didn't want to convey hostility, he wasn't going to cower, either. These people probably admired courage, and he had his pride, after all. He took sure steps as he was led closer to the couple, except he faltered a moment when he spied a familiar face in the crowd. There was Mica, as he'd hoped. There was only a moment for him to make eye contact, but doing so bolstered his spirits. There was something about that boy… Well, it was a good reminder that he still lived when his cock stirred some. He flashed a grin at Mica in the hopes that he might wipe away the look of worry he saw on the boy's beautiful face. If his fate was as ugly as he feared, he also hoped Mica would leave before he witnessed it.

A shove from the lead warrior had Geoff tumbling to his knees. He hit the hard-packed earth with a bone-jarring force. The position didn't bother him, but he straightened his torso immediately so as to not cower. He looked the chief in the eye and waited for the man to speak. This was his turf, after all. Geoff had no rights and could only hope to make his case to be allowed to continue on his journey. Although diplomacy wasn't his strong suit, this situation struck him rather as one soldier talking to another. Fighting men could be more dispassionate than courtiers and be counted on to make strategically logical decisions. At least, that was his experience. Who knew what these people were like? He only had his interaction with Mica to go by, yet the boy's gentle demeanor had to have come from somewhere.

The chief glared down at him and thumbed his chest. "Chief Chayton of the People, I am. To our land comes who?"

It took Geoff a moment to realize he was being asked the question and not the warrior hovering over his back. Geoff inclined his head. "I am Sir Geoffrey Arbuthnott of Moorcondia."

"Many names you have and oddly you speak. Chief you are?"

"No, sir. I am a...warrior of my chief." He spoke slowly in order to make it easier for the man to adjust to his cadence and syntax. His experience with Mica reassured him that it would happen quickly and easily enough.

The man's scowl deepened. "Raider, you are."

"No, sir. We are merely on a journey to explore lands we know nothing about. Our interest is to acquire knowledge, not to invade the territory of others." Even as he explained himself, he knew that in the man's place, it could easily mean he was on an advanced scouting mission in order to test the vulnerabilities of other people. Damn Professor Johns for his curiosity, and damn himself for not putting his foot down about entering the canyon.

Licking his dry lips, he tried to find better words. "We were curious about your way of life. It fascinates us that you dwell within the rock. You have nothing that we want to steal from you. Everything you have, we have more of—supplies, weapons and food. And they are as of the same good quality, if not better." He inwardly winced at his own strategy. Was insulting one's captor a good idea? Was he straddling the line between being impressive and taunting? It was impossible for him to know, so he just kept his gaze fixed on the chief and waited for a response.

The man surprised him by turning to the woman at his side. "As shaman of the People, what say you, sister?"

The woman stared down at him with a weird stillness, her eyelids fluttering and a strange humming noise passing her lips. Then she went still, and her gaze narrowed. "Dangerous he is, but truth he speaks."

Relief swept through Geoff. Whoever and whatever this woman was, besides the chief's sister, her words clearly held weight. He could see it in the chief's eyes. His next words, however, dashed Geoff's hopes.

"Truth or no, aggression I cannot accept." He pointed his finger at Geoff. "Your life you forfeit. To your men, mercy I show. Go they may." His words sent low murmurs through the crowd.

His bowels turned watery, but that was a momentary reaction. He was a soldier and understood death was always on the horizon. If killing him fulfilled some kind of custom or made the chief stronger in the eyes of his people, then so be it. Sparing his men was solace enough—not that he could be sure of that.

He stiffened his spine. "I accept your edict as to my fate. How do I know you will let my men go?"

There was a collective gasp among the onlookers. The chief reared back as if he'd been struck. "Lie I do not! Kill them I can, regardless. No purpose would lying make."

Well, he had him there. There really was no point in the man promising to let the others go when he already had them pinned down. It wasn't as if he needed Geoff's cooperation in anything. He sighed. "Fair point."

The chief showed no signs of glee at his pronouncement. He looked resigned, if not sad, at his duty—not that his feelings mattered to Geoff's future. "To the sun rising from the Earth Mother's embrace, spill your blood we will."

Dawn. Great, he had the whole night to fret over his fate. He'd rather be done with it. Executions always were a bit of a spectacle, he supposed. The more drama the better consequences sunk into those contemplating bad deeds. As there was nothing to say, he remained silent until two warriors grabbed him on both sides and hauled him to his feet. He didn't fight them or his fate. If this was the price to be paid to protect Lucas, Johns and the others, he had no choice but to accept that his life was coming to an end.

* * * *

Mica waited until the moon fully replaced her sister, sun, before daring to go to the pen where Geoff was being held. He made sure to keep his head up and his pace slow, so as not to call attention to himself. He didn't want to give anyone a chance to object to what he was doing, and in fairness to himself, no one had said he couldn't visit the prisoner or bring him nourishment. If he acted as if he had the right to do so, he hoped he wouldn't be questioned. As the nephew of the chief and the son of the shaman, he did hold a certain amount of status among the People. His movements weren't normally questioned, and he had to believe this night would be no different.

Still, as he approached the warriors guarding Geoff, he lifted his chin and adopted an air of bravado that belied his nerves. "Water and food for the prisoner I bring." He stared down the two men, warriors barely passed their manhood ceremony and therefore, stuck with the unenviable task of guarding the prisoner. He'd grown up with them both and knew they weren't prone to meanness.

One of them merely shrugged and gestured toward where Geoff sat with hands and feet bound. He was leaning with his back against the wicker fence, and his head was tipped back as he gazed up at the night sky. When Mica approached, however, he turned to stare at him. A wide smile stretched his face, his white teeth showing in the gloom of the perimeter torches. The sight of the man's joy at seeing him did funny things to Mica's gut, and his stride hitched a moment. Seeing the man up close once more reminded him of the impact this stranger had on him. Desire warred with his fear over Geoff's fate, making his stomach churn and his head swim with the intensity of his emotions. No one had ever had this kind of effect on him before. He didn't know what to do with it.

He put away his feelings and concentrated on the task at hand. How he felt about Geoff really didn't matter. The man deserved some comfort on his last night, as anyone would. Mica knelt beside the fence and glanced up at Geoff. "Some food and water I have brought. Want them, do you?"

"Yes, please, and thank you." There was a huskiness to the stranger's voice, as if he hadn't been given anything to drink in a while.

When Mica passed the flask he held through the pickets between them, Geoff took it and greedily drank.

"Hah," the man said when he was finished. "I was damnably thirsty, I must admit."

Pleased with his reception, Mica unwrapped the piece of flatbread he'd folded around some cheese. "Eat you must."

Geoff hesitated only a second before trading the flask for the food. "I suppose I should keep up my strength. Executions are a hard business." He bit off a chunk and grinned around his mouthful.

Mica dropped his gaze again. "Joke, you should not."

Geoff grunted and swallowed. "I don't see why. Not that I've had any previous experience, mind you, but levity seems like a better idea than crying." He took another bite.

Not sure how to respond, Mica dared to slip a hand through the fencing and put it on Geoff's thigh. "Sorry I am. Heed me you did not." An anger that he'd tamped down since Geoff had been brought into the village rose within him. Why hadn't the man kept to the course that led away from the village?

"You're right about that. If I were you, I'd be mad, too. I hate the idea I might have gotten you in trouble. Has anyone asked you awkward questions about me?"

Mica shook his head. "No. And misunderstand me you have. Worry for you, not for myself I do."

"Ah." Geoff popped the last of the food into his mouth and, as he chewed, he placed his hand on top of Mica's. It was warm and exuded strength without using any pressure. "I won't tell you not to. But at least I've had a chance to see you again. That's some good, from my perspective, among the obvious bad."

With a quick glance to make sure the guards paid them no attention, Mica shuffled as close to the fence as he could manage and pressed his face against it. "Pleasure at seeing you as well I have. Your death I cannot stand." His voice caught and he had to blink back sudden tears. How had this stranger gotten under his skin so quickly?

Geoff tugged Mica's hand closer to him. "Don't cry on my account. The decisions that led me to this fate were mine alone, and it is my duty to take the punishment so that my men can go free." He paused. "Your chief is telling the truth, is he not, that the others won't be harmed?"

Mica sniffed. "Yes. Truth that is. Honorable my uncle is."

"Your uncle? Does that mean the shaman is your mother?" When Mica nodded, the man chuckled. "Well, that's interesting but hardly matters. I would have saved you, no matter what. Did you get in much trouble over your absence?"

"No." A thought occurred to him, one that should have earlier than this. "Tell them I will and mercy I will ask for. For you," he clarified. "A life for a life." He had no idea whether it would matter to the chief that Geoff had saved his life. No doubt he would get in serious trouble for being so foolish as to keep to himself the news about the strangers on the People's land. And it might make no difference to Geoff's execution. It was still worth the risk.

Geoff dashed his hopes. "No. You won't say anything, Mica. Given how upset your people are about me and my men being here, I have to assume you will be in trouble for withholding that information from the others. Tell me I'm wrong."

"Cannot." Mica dropped his chin.

Geoff pressed his face close to the fence. "Whatever punishment that might entail, I won't risk it. Chances are your chief won't give a damn about my pulling you out of that quicksand. Even if he sees it as an act of kindness, it doesn't mean I didn't have bad intent toward the rest of you. My death won't be easier knowing you suffer some terrible fate."

"A beating maybe." Mica had witnessed other men being lashed with leather strips. The pain and humiliation of it wasn't something he dismissed as trivial, yet it would be nothing compared to Geoff losing his life.

Geoff squeezed his hand. "The thought of someone marring your lovely skin brings me no relief, and I truly don't think it will improve my fate. Look at me, Mica." When he raised his eyes, Geoff gave him a heated look. "You are the most beautiful boy I've ever seen. I will go to my death with a vision of your face in my mind. It will help. Promise me you'll say nothing."

Mica could hear the fierceness in the man's tone and not wanting to cause Geoff any more worry, he agreed. "Promise."

They were both quiet for a while, simply sitting and holding hands. Mica thought he could stay the whole night there, although he knew he wouldn't be permitted to. His parents would come looking for him if he didn't return soon.

"I hate to ask." Geoff's voice was low. "How…um, what method of execution do your people use?"

Mica couldn't bring himself to say the words. Instead, he chopped the back of his neck with the side of his hand.

"Ah. A classic method and quick, if done right. Let's hope the ax is a sharp one, then."

Mica only nodded. He'd never seen anyone punished in this most severe way, although a warrior had been when Mica was a child. There were few reasons for an execution, and that man had beaten his wife to death while drunk and enraged—an unpardonable transgression in the eyes of the Earth Mother. And because only adults were called to witness public punishment, he hadn't seen it himself and only knew what he'd been told. The Earth Mother demanded a quick, clean spilling of blood, no matter what, though. At least Geoff wouldn't suffer—much.

"I need one more promise, Mica."

"Anything." He stared into Geoff's eyes, trying to memorize every detail.

"Don't come to watch it." He overrode Mica before he could even open his mouth. "Please. It won't help me, and I want you to remember me—if you even do with the passage of time—as I was the night we spent together. It was only talking and yet, it was one of the best experiences of my life. Like I said, I'll picture you as I go, as you are right now."

Geoff pressed his mouth into a gap in the pickets, his invitation obvious. Mica didn't hesitate to do the same, and although it was the barest of touches, their lips met. The brief contact sent heat coursing through him. He shuddered and had to bite back a mew of disappointment when Geoff pulled away.

"What you do to me, my desert boy." Geoff pressed their still clasped hands against his groin. The hardness there sent another jolt through him. "It seems even impending death can't dissuade me from wanting you. It's not to be, though, is it? And we will start to attract too much attention. That won't be good for your standing in the community, I'm sure." He released Mica's hand. "You should go now."

Mica didn't want to. He fought the urge to pull the fence down with his bare hands so he could crawl into Geoff's lap and finish what they'd started. But he knew the man was right. A quick look over his shoulder told him one of the guards was already staring at them. He didn't care for himself, but he didn't want to make things harder on Geoff.

He reluctantly got to his feet. "Go I will."

"And stay away tomorrow, yes?"

"Yes."

He turned, and with dragging feet, made his way home. He didn't look back, even though he really wanted to. It wasn't so much the guards he feared. It was more that he didn't want Geoff to see the lie in his face. He would go to the execution because he wanted Geoff to have more than a memory to soothe him. The crowd watching him would be quiet because the solemnity of it required respect. To a person, though, they would welcome the death of a presumed enemy. Geoff didn't deserve to die at all, let alone among purely hostile witnesses. Mica wanted the last thing the man saw to be the face of someone who cared for him.

Chapter Four

Perhaps Mica had no right to feel pride at the way in which Geoff approached his death with stoicism. As he was led onto the sacrificial dais with his hands tied behind his back and two warriors gripping his arms, he showed no fear in his expression. He held his head high, as well, his expression neutral, with no visible emotion. His demeanor didn't crack, either, as he was made to kneel with more force than necessary. It had to have hurt when his knees met the unyielding stone floor, yet he didn't grimace or cry out. There was not so much as a flicker of discomfort as he gazed out at those gathered to see something unusual. Normally, an old animal would be killed here during festivals as an offering to the Earth Mother. A man losing his head was rare, and it was dismaying to know that so many of the People feared this stranger that they wanted to witness his blood spilt.

Mica had pushed his way to the front of the crowd in order for Geoff to be able to look right at him. When the man's gaze landed on him, his expression turned grim—the only crack in his facade. He'd asked Mica, after all, to not come. Mica could only give him a smile and a nod to demonstrate his affection and hopefully communicate that he wanted to give Geoff some comfort. After a moment, Geoff returned the smile briefly before looking down. The thin, low-slung stone altar where his neck would rest when the time came was the only thing in his line of vision. As Mica's mother began to speak the necessary words for the occasion, he couldn't help wishing that Geoff would gaze at him again, but that was selfish thinking. The man had a right to do whatever made these last few minutes of his life bearable.

"Handsome he is. Big and strong, too," a woman nearby said.

"Yes," her companion agreed. "Marry him I would under the ancient rite but mad my husband would be."

The two women giggled, but Mica's mind was already racing with the comments. He knew what they were referring to. It was an old custom that must have meant more back when executions might have been common. He knew there had been such a time. In his lifetime, death for one's enemies occurred with hot-blooded fighting. Taking prisoners was unheard of. If they didn't die, they fled, and that was good enough for the People. Those among them that committed offenses were forced to pay restitution through labor or were banished if considered incorrigible. In the past, however, there had been a belief that if a woman was willing to take on the rehabilitation of a man, she only had to offer him marriage to halt the execution. How often that had happened was unknown to him. He could imagine it hadn't been very, yet there were those among the People that could claim forefathers from other tribes. It was a rule that could be used still — if he dared.

Mica's heart leaped with the thought. It was madness on a basic level, yet it also felt right in his heart. Geoff didn't deserve to die, no matter the provocation. He was a good man and should be given the chance to live — that was assuming the chief and the shaman would accept the idea of a man offering the marriage salvation. Maybe the idea of being married to Mica wouldn't appeal to Geoff anyway, and that thought gave Mica an ache in his chest. And he supposed the condemned man could choose to refuse the offer and accept death instead. He hoped that Geoff wouldn't do so, but he really didn't know him very well. If he considered what it would mean to tie himself to a stranger, he might choose to stay silent. His life could change for the worse if he went ahead with the idea.

The risk can I take?

The answer came to him in the next instant when his mother finished her incantation and one of the warriors forced Geoff to place his head on the chopping block while the other raised a stone ax. The crowd grew completely silent. It felt as if they collectively held their breath.

Mica propelled himself forward. "Wait!" All eyes turned to him, and the executioner stayed his hand. He swallowed hard to raise spit within his dry mouth. He looked the chief in the eye and straightened as much as he could. "Invoking the ancient offer of marriage I am — the prisoner to spare."

There was a gasp, then voices murmured throughout the crowd until the chief held up his hand.

"What nonsense you speak?"

Mica stiffened his spine under the man's intimidating glare. "Nonsense it is not. With marriage, save this man's life I do."

There was more restless talk among the People while the chief went to confer with the shaman. From her expression, his mother was not happy at this turn of events. She shot him a glare before giving her brother her attention. Their voices were too low to carry, although their gestures showed how animated their discussion was. Mica knew his mother held the key to whether this would work. This issue undoubtedly was not whether the marriage right existed but whether a man could make the offer to another man. To his knowledge, men didn't form families with each other, although there were a couple of older men who lived together and had for most of their life. No one thought anything of it, and surely that kind of commitment was a type of marriage. If his mother said the Earth Mother sanctioned such a union, the matter would be settled. He feared she wouldn't, if for no other reason than he suspected her pronouncements had more to do with how she thought and not something the Earth Mother whispered in her ear.

Mica switched his attention to Geoff, preferring to look at him instead of the others. Geoff lifted his head enough to look back at him. His expression was hard to read, yet he mouthed words easy enough to understand.

What are you doing?

Mica mouthed a response. *Trust me you will. Please.*

His attention was taken before he and Geoff could say anything more when the chief and the shaman returned to the center of the dais. Once more, the chief held up his hand to silence the onlookers.

The man didn't look happy. "Clear the law is. A marriage offer by a man made is permitted because a prohibition on it exists not." He let that pronouncement sink in with everyone before gesturing for the executioner to step back and the other warrior to raise Geoff to his feet. "Accept Mica as your wife do you?" he asked of Geoff.

The poor man stood silent for a few seconds, blinking and frowning. Then he glanced at Mica and his mouth spread into a grin. "Yes."

Mica was nearly giddy with relief. It had worked! He had saved Geoff's life, and soon he would be bound to this man for the rest of his life. The marriage rite would probably occur immediately so that the previously condemned man didn't walk among the People for a moment longer without being one of them. It was a scary prospect for his life to change so quickly and profoundly, but also an exciting one. That very night he'd finally be able to find pleasure in the arms of another man. The mere thought of it made his skin tingle and his cock harden. He had to work at keeping his arousal out of his expression. He tried, instead, to appear solemn, grown-up and understanding of the enormous responsibility he'd just accepted. Unsure of what he was expected to do, Mica took a step forward to join Geoff on the dais.

"Stop!"

Everyone's attention was taken by Lonan pushing through the crowd to stand beside Mica. His expression was bordering on fury as he flicked his gaze in Mica's direction, although he schooled his face into a more neutral look when he addressed the chief.

He pointed at Mica. "Marry he cannot as a child he remains still. No manhood initiation has he had."

Crap. In the heat of the moment when he'd made his offer, he hadn't considered his eligibility. Although it was true that he hadn't had his official initiation, he was by all other measures an adult. The ordeal of the manhood initiation, followed by the celebration that would mark him as an adult, he'd yet to go through. It was a crucial event for their customs but surely it couldn't change what had already been agreed to.

His mother stepped forward, her mouth in a firm line. However she might feel about Mica's marriage ploy, she didn't like Lonan interfering with her authority. "Truth you speak, but easily rectified this problem is." She flicked her gaze to Mica before addressing the chief directly. "Tonight shall my son's initiation commence. Marry he will when completed it is."

Mica's father appeared suddenly by his side. For once, Lye wasn't in his arms. No young children were allowed at an execution, after all, even those unable to understand what was happening. The man fairly vibrated with anger as he stood with legs planted wide and his arms folded, which Mica could only assume was driven by his boldness and intent to become an interloper's wife and not a husband of a woman of the People. But however the man might feel about his son marrying another man, he also never questioned his wife's judgment as shaman.

"Agree I do," he proclaimed, "by the right of the father I am."

Mica felt relief. Between his parents, his effort to marry Geoff was going to succeed. He was grateful for the support. It was even more remarkable because he was certain neither of them liked the idea of welcoming this stranger man into their family.

The chief nodded once. "Done then."

Lonan's mouth tightened as he turned his attention to Mica's father. "His guide I will be."

Mica's stomach dropped at the pronouncement. The last thing he wanted was to be stuck deep inside the mountain where his life skills and courage would be tested with this man. A guide was supposed to be a man he could trust, someone encouraging him as he strove for survival and for the inner peace that came from being a man whose strength was forged in an unknown environment.

Mica was shaking his head before he even managed to speak up. "No." He also turned to his father, who more than anyone had the final say in how his initiation would occur. "My choice of guide I have, yes?" When his father inclined his head in agreement, Mica dug down deep once more for the strength he needed to voice his desires. "A warrior it must be, so him I choose." He pointed at Geoff.

Facing certain death had not been easy, but Geoff had allowed himself to be brought to his slaughter without protest. It had been a matter of pride, and accepting that, nothing he did would alter the outcome of his fate. Seeing Mica front in center of the crowd, his lovely face bearing both sad eyes and a clear effort to soothe Geoff's nerves, had nearly undone him. There was no question that despite his promise otherwise, the boy had come to support him in his final moments — and not out of the kind of lurid curiosity that attracted people to executions. Any wobbling of his resolve had been banished in his effort to not add to the boy's obvious distress.

This new turn of events, in which agreeing to marry Mica had apparently spared his life, was causing his brain to seize with confusion while the rest of his body sparked with anticipation. It made no sense to him that simply having someone step up to offer themselves in marriage was enough to turn him from deadly enemy to new member of their society. And whatever belief there was in the power of a woman to alter a man's behavior, it was even more bizarre that Mica's people had quickly accepted that this custom could apply to a male bride, as well. The furtive and furious discussion between the chief and the shaman had confirmed that this was a novel situation. He was grateful, certainly, for being saved, but he also couldn't help worrying what it would mean to be married to Mica. He wanted the boy, to be sure, but sex was one thing. A lifetime commitment was another. *Can I really take him on as a wife and do right by him?* There was no choice. He had to. That was the decision he'd made the moment when he'd agreed. The alternative was to put his head back on the block.

And all that worry was nothing compared to his need to protect the boy. If he was following the discussion correctly, some kind of ceremony was necessary to usher Mica officially into adulthood. While he had no idea what was involved, it was clear that he was to be accompanied by a man, and it was equally obvious that the warrior offering to fulfill that role was offensive to the boy. No surprise, given how Geoff had had the same reaction when the man had ambushed him. Mica's expression revealed to him, however, that not only did the boy dislike this warrior, he was afraid of him — as well he should be. The way the man looked at Mica was predatory. And his bride-to-be was looking to him for protection.

Fierceness rose in him. "I accept whatever role there is under your customs for this guide."

The crowd that had gathered watched avidly as the warrior sputtered out his objection. They all practically leaned forward as one to catch whatever the chief and the man who was Mica's father were discussing about this situation. There was a short, low exchange between the two men, one that they kept between them, shutting out the asshole warrior who tried to insert himself. Geoff didn't even try to make out what was being said. It was all so much noise as far as he was concerned. Instead, he focused his attention on Mica, trying to silently reassure him that all would be well because it *would* be. He'd be damned if he accepted Mica being at the mercy for even a moment of a man who obviously wanted the boy for himself.

The chief and the father broke off their talk to come and stand on either side of him. They eyed him as if he were a carcass hanging in a market stall. He stared them both in the eye, not to be challenging but to make sure they knew he was no one to trifle with. Whatever might be expected of him during this ceremony for Mica, it was obviously something that required a man with strength, skill and courage. He had all those qualities in abundance, if he said so himself. Of that, he had no doubt, and using them to protect Mica would be his great honor...and pleasure. The idea that he would soon be able to bed the boy caused his groin to tighten and his blood to thicken with passion. As hungry and thirsty as he was at the moment, his desire for the boy had no trouble rising to the surface and overriding all his other needs.

Mica's father grasped his upper arm and squeezed. "Strong warrior you are. Skills you have to survive?"

Geoff gave the man a bland stare. "If I didn't, my king wouldn't have chosen me for this expedition. Whatever the boy needs during this initiation, he will have it from me."

Mica's father narrowed his gaze and dug his fingers into Geoff's biceps. "Touch him before the marriage you will not."

Gritting his teeth against the pain, Geoff inclined his head. "As you say, sir. I will not dishonor him. The same cannot be said, I dare say, about *him*." He jutted his chin toward the warrior who remained by the edge of the dais, scowling.

Releasing his grip, Mica's father took a step back. "Keen your eyes are, too." To the chief, he added, "Accept him I do." His voice was loud enough to carry to all ears.

The chief gave a curt nod to the warrior standing next to Geoff. The next thing he knew, the ropes binding his wrists fell away. He stood rubbing the circulation back into his hands and waited for whatever was to come next. He hoped it involved having some time alone with Mica. His promise to the father notwithstanding, he figured he and the boy deserved to show each other a bit of affection. The chief dashed his hopes with his next pronouncement.

"Imprisoned until the initiation you shall stay, as a member of the People you are not yet." He gestured with his head for Geoff to be led away.

As he descended the dais, Mica came up to him and his escorts, forcing them to stop. "Come with him I will. My right it is as my husband he is to be," he said to the chief.

The man gestured in agreement with his intent. With a shy smile, Mica wasted no time stepping to Geoff's side and taking his hand. The touch was both soothing and arousing. The heightened emotions caused by his near death could explain Geoff's painfully hard cock, but he knew that touching Mica was the bigger catalyst. As they walked back to the pen where he'd been kept, he allowed himself to enjoy the contact with the boy and imagined how much sweeter it would be when they were finally alone — and naked. He would take his time to explore every inch of the delectable body. He'd already tasted the boy's lips and had no doubt the rest of him would be just as sweet.

They were forced apart when they reached the pen, the guards pushing Geoff inside, although without the same vigor as they'd used previously. Mica stood by the pickets on the outside, pouting for a moment. His obvious ire at the separation was adorable. Then he abruptly turned and strode away.

Geoff kept the boy in his sights so was not surprised when he returned with a water skin in his hands. Geoff walked to the far back of the pen where there was a splinter of shade from an overhanging rock and sat heavily. Now that the drama of the morning was over, his legs felt weaker than he would have liked. He was strong when he needed to be but not even a seasoned soldier such as himself was immune from the inherent fear that came from a near-death experience. When Mica shoved the skin through the pickets, Geoff gratefully took it and gulped down the surprisingly cool water.

He sighed once he'd had his fill and leaned against the back of the pen. "Thank you…for everything."

Mica squatted with his hands dangling between his legs. "Angry you are not?"

"Angry?" Geoff chuckled. "At what? Your saving my life?" He shook his head. "That would be very churlish of me. Besides, the chance to bed you is very appealing."

Mica's high cheek bones turned a darker shade, and he dropped his gaze. "Want you as well, I do."

"Good. I hope enough to bind yourself to me for the rest of your life. It's a big decision, Mica, and one that I trust you didn't make on the spur of the moment because you hated to see me die." He could tell by the way the boy's eyes went wide that he'd hit on the truth. "Oh, Mica. Think it through more and take back your offer if you want. My life isn't worth your misery."

The boy's expression turned mulish. "No. Want you I do," he repeated before standing. "Hungry are you?" He shook his head. "Foolish question. Food I will bring."

"Mica, we must talk."

When Geoff tried to grab the boy's hand through the picket, he stepped out of reach. Then he was gone, leaving Geoff feeling uneasy now that he'd had a chance to consider what all this meant. Not being executed was certainly a desirable outcome, but he didn't want his freedom to come with the price of Mica being tied to a man he didn't want for more than a quick roll on a pallet or whatever the people used for a bed.

He was tired, though, having not slept all night, trying to grab as much life as he could. Now, his eyes drooped, and he gave into the need to sleep, if only for a little while. He woke with a start at the sound of Mica returning. The boy sat cross-legged in the spot he'd crouched in before. He held a sack and, placing it on the ground, began to take out what looked and smelled like a veritable feast to Geoff's hungry body.

There was bread, cheese and dried meat, followed by figs and roasted, sugared seeds of some kind. Geoff ate with his usual hearty appetite, determined to stop fretting about the idea of marriage and instead, focus on what this manhood initiation involved. If he could get Mica through that, the rest could be handled. Perhaps the best thing he could do for the boy was to secure him with the status of being a warrior's wife and leave him to live with his people while he continued on his way to meet up with Lucas and the others. It was a logical plan, except that the thought of leaving the boy behind was like a stab to both his gut and his heart.

Don't be ridiculous. I need to reason this problem through.

The first thing at hand was the upcoming initiation. Geoff licked his sticky finger and thumb. "Tell me what you do to become a man and what my role is as a guide."

Mica had silently watched him consume every morsel of food, a look of satisfaction on his face. Now he turned thoughtful. "Survive for three nights in the mountain I must." He looked up the cliffside and pointed. "Up there we go, past the crops and the dwellings into the belly of the Earth Mother's highest place."

Geoff pictured the craggy wall of rock soaring into the sky and past the clouds. "Have you ever been inside?"

Mica's eyes widened. "No. Sacred it is, for ceremonies only."

Geoff emptied the skin of water before asking another question. "Are you allowed to bring anything with you?"

Mica nodded, a bit of excitement showing in his expression now. "A knife, rope and flint stone."

"No water or food?"

Mica shook his head. "Provide for you the Earth Mother does. Find it and use it I must." The boy shrugged. "Little information is given. My wits I must use, no matter what I find."

"Ah." So rudimentary survival skills were tested and in an environment that boys wouldn't be used to. It didn't sound so bad. "And what am I supposed to do?"

"Watch. On my skills you report. Save me if something stupid I do." He hung his head as if he'd already failed. "Shameful it would be."

Geoff would have laughed if Mica hadn't looked so sad. Instead, he reached to clasp his hand. "You will be fine, I'm sure. Anyone who can go about the desert alone is a survivor."

Mica frowned. "Different is the mountain, and quicksand I fell into. Remember you should."

Now Geoff did laugh. "Ah yes, and I'm glad of it. Otherwise, we'd never have met. And I don't expect that's a good example of your skills."

Mica looked at him from under his lashes. "With you as guide, afraid I am not."

Touched, Geoff scooted as close to the boy as the pickets would allow. He raised Mica's hand and kissed the inside of his wrist. "I won't let anything bad happen to you."

"Know that I do." Mica pressed his face into the fence. "Kiss me?"

How could Geoff refuse such a lovely request? A quick glance told him that no one paid them any mind. The morning's entertainment hadn't changed the fact that everyone in the village had chores to do. The guards weren't even giving the pretext of watching him. They squatted in front of the fence gate, playing some kind of dice-like game with colored pebbles.

He met Mica's mouth but had to satisfy them both with a simple sliding of their lips. It wasn't nearly enough. He wanted to deepen the kiss and taste more of the boy. Because that wasn't possible, he did something even bolder. Snaking his free hand between the pickets, he ran it up and under Mica's beaded vest. The skin was warm and surprisingly soft. When he rubbed one nipple with his thumb, he was rewarded by Mica moaning low and softly — for his ears only. The boy arched into the touch, a silent plea for more. Geoff obliged, plucking at both nipples with a firm grip. The boy shuddered and his breath began to labor. Geoff didn't have to break the kiss to look down to know that Mica was aroused and getting close to the edge already.

Wanting the encounter to last and ignoring his own painful erection, Geoff slid his hand down Mica's flat stomach and pushed his fingers past the waistband. There was more covering him beneath the kilt, cupping him tightly. Still, he could feel the tip of the boy's cock had managed to escape. He made Mica jump when he swept his nails over the head. It wouldn't take much to cause the boy to climax. But Geoff wanted to grab a better handful. He angled his body to shield Mica from prying eyes and pulled his hand back in order to slide it up the boy's thigh instead. He encountered a strip of leather acting as the smallest of small clothes. It took nothing to get past it. His reward was to find a hard, hot shaft to wrap his fingers around.

Mica whimpered against Geoff's lips but didn't move away. If anything, he leaned against the fence more, the wicker groaning with the pressure. It hardly mattered. The worst that could happen was the section of the fence could collapse and Mica would land in Geoff's lap. He couldn't work up too much concern. Mica was going to be his wife, after all, and the prohibition on not touching him had been a bit lacking in specifics. He was willing to argue with a straight face to Mica's father that he'd complied by not touching the boy with his own dick.

It hardly mattered in any event. It only took a few strokes before Mica's dick jerked and cum spilled over Geoff's hand. Mica puffed hot breaths past Geoff's lips and his body continued to shudder until the orgasm subsided. When it had, Geoff reluctantly pulled his hand free and broke off the kiss. As he sat back, he kept his gaze on Mica. Then he made a show for his eyes only of licking the cum off his fingers as he'd done with the sticky remnants of the sugared seeds. To his mind, they were equally delicious, but it was Mica's wide-eyed stare that made the gesture worth it.

"Never doubt I want you, my dear."

"I do not." Mica reached for him. "Touch you may I?"

Oh, such a temptation, but they'd pushed the boundaries of propriety as it was. "A delightful offer, but I'm fine. I could use some sleep, truth be told." In emphasis, a yawn overtook him. "Go and do whatever you must to prepare for tonight. I shall dream of you," he added with as much a gleam in his eyes as he could manage, given his fatigue.

Mica pushed out his lower lip. "Not fair."

"Life seldom is, but I promise you when this is over, you'll be very happy with the waiting. It makes the having that much better."

That seemed to do the trick. Mica blew him a kiss, then stood and walked away. Geoff allowed himself the pleasure of watching the boy's fetching ass retreat before giving in to the unbearable fatigue and slipping into sleep.

Chapter Five

Mica had washed up at the stables in order to hide what he'd done with Geoff as best he could. Rather what Geoff — his future husband — had done *to* him. He couldn't bear thinking about it because it only served to arouse him more. If so much pleasure could be had from a man's hand, how much better would it be when it was a cock? His sphincter clenched at the mere thought, but the sight of his father waiting for him outside the entrance to their home did a perfect job of deflating his desire. As usual, the man held Lye, and instead of making him sad or jealous, Mica was glad his father had the chance for the kind of son he wanted. Mica had never been that for him, and now with his impending marriage to another man, whatever hopes his father might have held about him were surely done to dust.

"For the initiation tonight, rest you must."

As per usual, Lye reached for Mica. This time, however, their father didn't let him go, as if Mica were already lost to them as a son and brother.

Mica hid his disappointment. Although he had no actual idea what Geoff had planned for them once they were husband and wife, Mica had to assume the man didn't intend to remain here and make a life among the People. He had too many responsibilities to his own kind. Would he leave soon after their wedding night to rejoin his men? *Probably.* And Mica's father likely assumed Mica would stay with his husband, because that's just what wives did.

Saying nothing, he merely nodded and headed inside.

His mother was before him in an instant, as if she too had been waiting. Her expression was extra grim. "Foolish you are. Becoming a *wife* — and to a stranger? Understand you I do not, but on the pallet made by you, you shall lie. On *his* pallet," she corrected with a shake of her head. "Fuck you he will, like a woman."

His mother's crudeness surprised him. Mica didn't let himself be cowed by it. Lifting his chin, he said, "Know that I do."

"No children you shall have."

"And that as well I know. For me that life you planned would never have pleased me. A man I want and always have."

That confession didn't change his mother's demeanor. She frowned more fiercely. "And go with him you will when he demands it?"

Alyn came up, a softer expression on her face. "No, true that is not. Stay with the People you both will, yes?"

Mica was pretty certain of the answer, yet didn't want to face the hurt his sister, at least, would suffer over his leaving. He shrugged. "Know not."

Except it was a lie, however much he meant it as a kindness. Unless some part of the People's custom that he didn't know about forced Geoff to stay in the village in order for the marriage to save him still from the execution, he would want to get back to his men as quickly as possible. He was under orders of his king and would keep up with his exploration, married or not. The only question was whether the man would merely perform the necessary duty of relieving Mica of his virginity then abandon him, or would he take Mica with him? Did he see Mica as an expedient way to avoid death and grab a bit of pleasure or was he willing to take on the extra burden of dragging his wife along?

The idea of traveling to unknown places thrilled Mica. He had never imagined his life could take such a turn. What had only been dreams of a different life would become his actual destiny. That didn't mean he wanted to leave his home and never look back. He would want to see his family again as much as possible. Although he barely knew the man, he was quite sure that Geoff would permit him to visit when they traveled through the People's land on the return trip. And Moorcondia didn't seem that far away, given what Geoff had told him that first night together. Surely Mica could come back now and again for the rest of his life, once he'd settled in Geoff's homeland. He had to believe that was true. The idea of not seeing his family day in and day out saddened him and made his stomach jitter. But he wouldn't be the first in such a situation. Women of the People left now and again to make new lives with other tribes. New blood for breeding was always welcome. If they could do it, so could he.

Alyn surprised him by grabbing him into a hug. "Miss you I will." She pulled back. "Glad I am that your guide Lonan will not be."

"As I am." The thought of being beyond the warrior's reach was a definite comfort, and he was sure Alyn would evade his embrace as well. She had the same strength as their mother, the strength of a shaman.

"Rest I must." Mica let go of his sister, and with a brief nod at his mother, left for his pallet.

As excited as he was about the initiation to come—and his marriage night after that—he had no trouble settling down. The ordeal of living through what might have been Geoff's execution and the languid residual feeling from the orgasm made it easy to drift off.

* * * *

Mica held his head high as he walked slowly beside his father up the cliffside steps, over the plateau and up to the yawning mouth of the mountain. People lined the way with torches held by other warriors to light the path. Behind him was Geoff, walking alone, no longer under guard and giving Mica the solid presence at his back that the guide was supposed to provide. There had been no chance to speak to him before the ceremony began. He wondered if anyone had bothered to give him any instructions. Not even Mica fully knew what the guide was supposed to do. It was not spoken of. Each boy becoming a man had to trust that others knew enough to make his initiation a success.

As he approached the cave opening, all he could see was the same darkness that had always been visible when he'd looked from afar. If he allowed it, his imagination could conjure up all kinds of monsters living inside. He gripped the hilt of the knife at his waist, gaining comfort from it, confident he could wield the weapon as well as anyone. Knowing that Geoff would be with him also bolstered his courage, of course. Perhaps he had no business putting so much faith in the man and his abilities after such a short acquaintance, yet he did. Part of him felt as if he'd been waiting for this man and no other for his entire life, that he'd known he was coming for him. Such was the power of Geoff's presence that Mica wasn't even fazed by the look of hatred in Lonan's eyes as he passed him. *In whatever expectations he has, let him stew.* There was nothing the warrior could do to Mica now.

At the mountain's mouth, the procession came to a halt. The chief and the shaman stood on either side of the entrance, each decked out in their ceremonial garb. There were words said by both of them. Mica had heard them before when it had been others' turns at initiation. It was all stylized entreaties to the Earth Mother to welcome him into her home, to guide him and protect him. In all honesty, Mica wasn't sure anyone was listening. Forget about whether there truly was an Earth Mother—a heresy he dared not even consider for more than a moment. It seemed doubtful that she would care about one event in the life of a boy of no significance. If he were to survive this test of manhood, it would be by his own wits and efforts…and those of Geoff, of course, although Mica was determined to need nothing from the man. He might not be made of the stuff of warriors, but Mica had his pride and wanted to succeed on his own.

The ceremonial incantations stopped abruptly, followed by silence. All eyes were on him, then on Geoff as well as Mica's father took a torch from someone and passed it over to him. Geoff took it with a solemn look and a brief nod. Whatever he might think of this initiation, Geoff was showing proper deference to Mica's father and the solemnity of the occasion. That demonstration of respect buoyed Mica's spirits. With each passing event, Geoff's character was coming into sharper relief. Life with this man would be good. Mica was sure of it.

Mica didn't wait to be told the next move was his. Taking a deep breath, he walked into the mouth of the cave. It took only a few steps before total darkness surrounded him. His heartbeat quickened, and he had to fight a sudden fright that threatened to overwhelm him. Then lightness arrived in the form of Geoff with his torch. The interior of the cave became visible. The dark rock and sandy floor were predictable and reassuringly boring. Nothing evil lurked in the shadowed corners that he could see, but the roof of the cave was made up of layers of what looked to be loose rock. It didn't have the deliberately carved appearance of the Peoples' dwellings, and it didn't seem possible that the covering would hold. Yet generations of men had been initiated through this place, so it had to be stable.

Putting aside thoughts of being buried alive, he started walking toward the tunnel leading deeper into the mountain. As someone who'd lived in a type of cave his whole life and not just riding free through the desert, he felt at ease with the familiar place. That was, until the walls narrowed enough that he could reach out on either side and touch them at the same time. He'd never been hemmed in like that before, and he knew a moment of fear that he was indeed being entombed alive. Mica stopped suddenly enough that Geoff brushed up against his back.

The man put a hand on his shoulder. "Are you all right?"

Mica licked his lips. "Foolish I am being. So little room there is."

"Being afraid of small spaces is not uncommon among my people. There is no shame in it. We are standing under an entire mountain, after all. Only someone truly foolish would be cavalier about that."

Mica looked over his shoulder. "Afraid you are not?"

Geoff offered him a smile. "Yes well, if it helps any, I wasn't too happy about the trek up here. Heights bother me."

"Truly?" Mica had no trouble with that. "Came you did, anyway."

"Because there was no choice. Fear is only a problem if it stops you from doing what you must." He paused and peered down into Mica's eyes. "We can turn back and spend the entire time in the first cavern."

Mica nearly laughed at the absurdity of the suggestion. "Cannot! Food and water we must find."

Geoff sighed. "You have me there. A few days without water would be very bad. But this is *your* initiation, Mica. I'm here to follow you and only interfere if it becomes urgent to do so in order to save you from serious harm or death."

Mica understood the import of his words. If he turned back and huddled at the front of the cave, Geoff would eventually find them water, at least to keep them alive until the others returned. His mind rebelled at the idea. He wasn't about to fail his test before it even began. It would mean being an adult for the rest of his life without being accepted as a fully grown man. That in-between state was not common, not in his lifetime in any event, and even if he left the People with Geoff, he would always know what he'd failed to accomplish, and the shame of it would always haunt him.

Straightening his shoulders, he continued without further discussion. Even this small amount of talk with Geoff felt as if it were against the rules. From this point forward, he needed to make decisions on his own and pretend that Geoff wasn't even there. As he went, he made use of the help the torch gave to see what useful things the cave offered for survival. Moss covered the walls in various places. Knowing that the torch wouldn't last forever to light their way, he stopped to scrape the relatively dry plant life and stuff it into the empty bag he'd been given, along with his knife, flint and short length of thin rope. It would make for a good substitute for portable light and also allow for a fire if he found a place where the smoke could vent properly.

Performing a useful task gave him greater confidence that he knew how to survive in this new environment. When he emerged into a new cavern, he took a moment to scour it for anything that might help his journey. Finding nothing other than more dark rock and sand, he pushed forward to the other side. There he found two tunnels. They were roughly of equal width, and neither gave away anything about what lay within. His sight being of no help, he strained to hear anything of interest and sniffed the air by each entrance. There was a faint odor of decay by one, and where there was that smell, it meant things lived and died within. It was a sign of possible food. His mind made up on his direction, he stopped to pick up small rocks and arrange them in an arrow pattern. When he came back, it would ensure that he didn't forget where to go to get out.

As he straightened, he caught Geoff's look of approval. Pleased that he'd done the right thing and that his future husband had noticed, he continued with even more assurance that he knew what to do. This new tunnel quickly widened, and the sound of rushing water caught his ears. A few twists and turns later, he stepped out into a massive cavern, wide and high, with shafts of light peeping through cracks in the ceiling and a large pool fueled by cascading water. Mica barked out a laugh and rushed forward to peer into the pool. It didn't take long to spy the fish within and cupping his hand, he sipped at the frigid liquid. It tasted amazing.

He grinned at Geoff over his shoulder. "To here is where I am meant to come. For many days survive we can."

Shoving the torch into the sandy floor to keep it upright, Geoff joined him to drink from the pool. "So it would seem." He glanced around. "All the comforts of home, I'd say."

Mica felt elated, even if finding this spot hadn't been all that hard. Perhaps it wasn't meant to be, that the true test was to persevere, even when the journey only seemed daunting. He'd always envied the girls' initiation because he'd have been confident in his ability to grind grain and prepare food. Those weren't traditional tasks for a boy to learn, but with only he and Alyn to rely on, his mother had taught him the same skills as she had his sister. They had seemed easy in comparison to the skills his father had schooled him in. He'd tried hard to be what his father had expected him to be, and now, he appreciated what the man had given him. He'd learned what he needed to succeed in his initiation—and then some. And he felt sorry for his sister and the other girls. They had it a lot harder than he did.

He rose. "Time to make camp and supper it is." He hadn't been allowed to eat anything when he'd woken toward twilight. And given the knots in his stomach from nervousness, he hadn't minded the prohibition. Now, he was starving.

Geoff stood as well, but only to go sit with his back against a large rock. He clasped his hands behind his neck. "Grilled fish will be most welcome."

Far from resenting the way the man was obviously expecting to be waited on, Mica's chest puffed at the idea. He was going to provide for his husband and make a comfortable home for them both. After feeding the man, he would try to coax him into more sex. He almost pitied the other boys who had to do this with someone that they didn't desire. His tie to Geoff made the entire venture more meaningful, and if he was clever, he might seduce this man completely. That possibility goosed him as nothing else did. Pulling off his boots, he planned how he was going to get those fish out of the water and over a fire.

* * * *

It had been hard at first for Geoff to sit back like the lord of the manor while Mica toiled to make camp and provide a meal from them both. But the boy was clearly confident at this point about what he was doing. Gone was the earlier near panic from being hemmed in by all that rock. He'd understood the natural rebellion of the mind over the buried-alive feel of the place. Only his harsh training as a soldier had made him immune from such fear. And while he'd been prepared to whisk Mica back to the mouth of the cave, he couldn't be prouder of how the boy had conquered his mounting terror and pressed on.

Every choice Mica had made had been the right one, too. His experience wandering the desert had served him well, even here in this unknown place. He'd chosen their route with care and obviously respected the hostile environment they were in. Finding this cavern on the first try had been a real coup. The boy had to be proud of himself. This place had all they needed to survive their time in the mountain. Geoff could see the remnants of many others having spent their initiations here.

Mica had waded into the pool and stabbed at fish with a spear cobbled together from the now-extinguished torch and his knife. He'd caught four, gutted them on a flat rock and cooked them on stones heated on top of the fire fueled by moss. The smoke twirled its way up and out through a fissure above the spot Mica had picked for their fire pit. Everything was perfect.

Mica is perfect.

The thought jolted Geoff enough that he placed one palm over his chest. It felt as if his heart had stopped before beating again with wild desire. The boy did make a tantalizing sight, crouched as he was to keep an eye on the cooking fish. He'd removed his kilt and vest before going into the water. All he wore was that bit of leather cloth that cupped his genitals with a thin strip running up the crack of his lovely, tight rump and around his waist. Geoff was nearly overrun by the urge to take the boy in hand and plunge into him at that very moment. The admonishment about touching from Mica's father stayed his hand, naturally, as did the idea of deflowering the boy in such an uncomfortable place. Mica deserved softness and tenderness, so no fucking. But as he'd done while he'd been locked up, he was willing to stretch the parameters of his promise. He wouldn't touch Mica with his dick until they were married.

That rationalization firmly set in his mind, he stood and stretched. "Is the fish nearly done?"

"Now, yes." Mica speared each piece with his knife and lay them on a flat rock he'd washed already. It was as clean a plate as they were going to get, and Geoff had eaten under far worse conditions.

He sat cross-legged next to Mica and picked at one fish with his fingers. This was not a species he was familiar with, but Mica appeared to be, as he hadn't hesitated to harvest them and was now enthusiastically stuffing his mouth with a fillet. Upon a tentative taste, Geoff found he liked it. The flesh was blandly sweet and satisfying to his tongue, which only meant that he'd enjoy his meal and those that would come over the next few days and not merely tolerate them for survival's sake. All in all, not a bad way to pass the time, although he worried that he hadn't been able to get word to Lucas about what was happening to him. He wasn't even sure the chief had recalled his warriors. No one seemed inclined to answer his questions, and he supposed that until he was probably wedded to Mica, he was still considered an enemy of sorts. There was nothing to be done about any of it, however, so he concentrated on the here and now.

As they ate, Geoff decided it was as good a time as any to ask questions that he had about their current situation. No one had said he couldn't glean information out of the boy. And really, what did the chief expect him to do, given that there had been precious little instructions about his role as a guide, other than to simply make sure Mica emerged alive? That part was obvious, regardless.

"How will we know when it's time to leave?" He glanced around the gloom. "It's not like we can mark the rising and setting of the sun from in here."

Mica swallowed and grabbed another fillet. "By my sleeping I will. The third time I wake, the end it will be."

"Hmm." That seemed like too much of a variable concept. Then again, as a soldier, he'd developed a fairly consistent rhythm of sleeping and waking himself. It was probably the same for Mica. His body would tell him when to bed down and when to rise again. It probably wasn't meant to be an exact period of time, anyway. As far as he could tell, Mica had already passed his initiation. The rest was probably for show, to give the event more drama.

They finished the rest of their meal in companionable silence. Mica licked the fingers of his eating hand one by one. The sight of it had the expected effect on Geoff. His cock hardened and his balls tightened with need. The boy appeared to have no idea how provocative he was being—until he looked in Geoff's direction. Mica froze with his lips wrapped around the pad of his thumb.

Mica's eyes widened and he slowly pulled the thumb out. "What?"

"Oh, I think you know." Geoff leaned over and stroked a finger down Mica's cheek.

The boy had no facial hair to speak of. None of the men in his village did. By contrast, his beard was starting to grow in, given how long he'd been away from his razor. It was at that scratchy stubble stage, and he worried about marring Mica's soft skin. He tugged him in for a kiss anyway. His desire was too great.

For the first time, they had privacy and nothing to impede them. Geoff took full advantage of the situation by embracing Mica in a hug and plunging his tongue past the boy's lips. He used Mica's single braid as leverage to angle his head to deepen the assault. It was as sweet a taste as he'd expected, Mica's mouth being warm and welcoming. And the boy didn't hesitate to melt into Geoff's arms. He uttered a breathy moan as he matched Geoff's intensity. Their hard cocks clashed against each other, despite the clothing confining them.

Geoff lifted Mica up enough to sit him on his lap, then began to hump into him. It wasn't nearly satisfying enough. Too many layers separated their shafts, muting the pleasure. Except maybe that was a good thing... Geoff felt his control slip almost immediately. His previous decision to wait until they were married to mount the boy flew out of his mind in the face of such exquisite arousal. He only had to turn Mica around, pull off that thong, untie his own laces and... *No, not like that, not with a virgin.*

Geoff bargained with himself by undoing Mica's thong with a quick tug at the tie keeping it in place. The boy's dick slapped against his belly, hot and needy. He cupped Mica's ass with both hands and made him buck. The boy shuddered, moaned and dug his fingers into Geoff's back. Geoff didn't have to be told that this was a new experience for him. Mica's reaction was too strong, and his sounds turned into desperate whimpering. Hearing his reaction alone egged on his own arousal. He pumped his hips to rub his dick against Mica's.

It was all over far too quickly. Mica toppled over the edge of orgasm first, groaning down Geoff's throat and shuddering into his chest. He scratched at Geoff's back, the bite of pain helping him climax as well. It was astoundingly powerful, as if he hadn't come in forever, as if it were his first time and discovering the pleasure to be had with his cock. The intensity caught him off guard, but he didn't dwell on it. Instead, he rode the wave and devoured as much of Mica as he could.

When Geoff broke the kiss to allow them both to catch their breath, Mica sighed and rested his head against Geoff's shoulder. "Wonderful that was."

Geoff stroked the boy's back and rocked him gently. "I heartily agree. You are a delight, Mica. And I fear it's going to be very hard for me to obey your father's orders to keep my hands off you. In fact, it already has been. I can't wait for this initiation to be over so that I can bed you properly — as your husband." Just saying that word sent a thrill through him.

"Talk of that again we should." Mica pulled back to look at him. "Sorry I am to force the marriage."

Geoff cupped his cheek. "Darling, there is no need to be. I'm happy to have kept my head on my shoulders, and marrying you is hardly a sacrifice. I thought I'd already made it clear to you that I've wanted you since the moment I first saw you. Committing myself to you is no hardship." A nagging worry did continue to push its way to the front of his brain, however. "I know you made the offer to save me, and I know we spoke of this before, but that was when our emotions were still running high. You've had time to consider our situation more, and I hope you are still not too unhappy with the prospect of becoming my wife?"

By way of an answer, Mica ran his hand down Geoff's chest and grasped his groin. He squeezed once with pressure somewhere between gentle and firm. "Dreamt of you I did...my whole life."

Geoff kissed him again, not as passionately, but slowly enough to explore Mica's mouth with more care. He laid his thumb against the boy's pulse point at this neck and smiled at the quick beat he found. It would take nothing for each of them to be ready for more pleasure. To make it easier on them, he freed his dick from its laces. Then he lay down on his back, barely noticing the rocky surface pressing into his skin, and maneuvered Mica to lie on top of him. It was the most comfortable resting place he could offer the boy, and it allowed him to run his hand up and down Mica's silky back. He even permitted himself to squeeze one buttock, although he resisted the urge to slide his finger between the crack. Once he breached the boy's hole, restraint would be nearly impossible.

Instead, he went back to what both worked and kept him on the right side of discretion. Sliding one hand between their bodies, he managed to clasp both of their cocks. The boy was fully aroused, and his older dick was valiantly trying to get there as well. He pumped the shafts together, using his thumb to swipe across both their cockheads. Pre-cum eased the way for his hand, and soon he was jerking with hard, sure strokes.

Once again, it took little to bring them to climax. Mica was so receptive to his touch, his body primed to orgasm under his control, that it gave Geoff a feeling of immense power. And with that came the nearly overwhelming sense of duty.

He kissed Mica gently before laying his head on his chest. "I shall always take great care of you."

"Know that I do," came the sleepy reply.

Geoff lay still with his arms wrapped around the boy who would soon be his wife, listening to the sound of his deep sleep. Something akin to pain stabbed at his heart. He wasn't sure what it was, having never experienced the feeling before. It was a type of ache, except it felt good, spreading a kind of warmth throughout his body. Then it hit him. *I'm falling in love with him.*

* * * *

A great rumbling sound accompanied by the ground shaking woke Geoff. In the way of all soldiers, he was instantly alert. He held onto a rousing Mica tightly as he strained to determine what was happening. He'd been to a far corner of Moorcondia when an earthquake had hit, a disturbing event. He thought that was what happened now, although he had no idea if that were truly the case. He glared up at the rock ceiling and tried not to imagine it collapsing on them. After what seemed like an eternal amount of time, the strange occurrence stopped abruptly. Geoff scanned the ceiling and was relieved to see that nothing appeared to have shifted. He tentatively sat up with Mica still in his arms.

The boy clutched at his shoulders. "What was that?"

"I don't know." Geoff got them standing and looked around for signs of trouble. "Perhaps nothing of note."

"Scared I am, Geoff."

As much as he liked the sound of his name on his boy's lips, Geoff put his own feelings aside and worked to reassure him. "We're fine. But we should go explore to see if we can figure out what has happened."

The small shafts of light that were visible up high were much brighter than they had been, proof that the sun was rising. So Mica's sleep patterns notwithstanding, the other men had known he had a way to keep track of time. There was just enough to make it easy to see around the cavern, even with the fire having nearly burned out. He eyed the tunnel from where they'd come. That way was still dark, however, and he was sure the sound had come from that direction.

"We must reconfigure a torch earlier than expected and go back in search of answers."

Mica turned away from him. "My job it is."

Geoff took him by the arm. "No, darling. This comes under the heading of an emergency. We work together on this."

Mica furrowed his brows for a moment. "Obey you I will, because experienced you are."

Another jolt of happiness pushed through the worry. It humbled him that Mica was willing to put himself in Geoff's hands so readily. He yanked off his shirt. "We'll use this to bundle moss for a new torch."

Geoff was no novice to making a torch out of whatever was at hand. Moss wrapped in his shirt and tied to the old shaft with some of Mica's rope made for a decent one. Mica used his flint to spark a fire, and while a good dose of oil would have helped with the flame and protected the shaft, it worked well enough.

And the stick of wood was long. As much as Geoff wanted to leave Mica behind, he dared not. If something more happened, he needed to be by the boy's side to protect him. If they got cut off from each other, there would be little hope of Geoff reaching his charge.

He took him by the hand and led the way. The journey back through the tunnel seemed faster than the one leading into the cavern. It was a trick of the mind, he knew, but he was still grateful for the illusion. It didn't take long to detect the fine mist of rock in the air. Learning the truth of their predicament was best done quickly. And Geoff was sure of what they would find, it was merely a matter of where. As they entered the previous cavern, he spotted the trouble only a moment before Mica did.

The boy gasped. "Trapped we are!"

As he eyed the mound of rocks blocking the entrance at the far end, Geoff's heart sank. Their worst fears had materialized. They were effectively buried alive within the great mountain.

Chapter Six

Geoff brushed the dust from his palms. "There is no way to dig our way out. The cave-in goes too far back, and each rock I move threatens to bring the others down on our heads if we try to make a tunnel through it. I'm sorry, darling. We need to find another exit. I don't suppose there's any lore among your people about that?"

Mica shook his head. "No." The boy was trying to be stoic, but the fear in his eyes was obvious.

Geoff went over to him and lay his hands on Mica's shoulders. "Don't worry. We'll figure it out." He jutted his chin at the tunnel they hadn't taken the first time. "We may have to try that route. First, though, we go back to the cavern and see if there is an escape route there."

He picked up the torch and taking Mica's hand, led them back to the first tunnel. "I'm going to douse this to preserve it. We should be able to make it by feel alone."

Mica said nothing, merely wrapped his arms around Geoff's waist as he smothered the flame in the dirt. The darkness was impenetrable this far from the cavern. Geoff put his free hand on the wall and let it guide him. He could feel Mica's trembling and understood that the same fear of being hemmed in had taken hold of him now that he couldn't see anything. Geoff had to balance his desire to make it a quick journey against the possibility of scaring his boy more by whisking him along. He breathed a sigh of relief when a crack of light showed through the darkness, and they finally arrived at the cavern.

"We didn't really look around much when we arrived because it didn't matter. There may be an opening somewhere."

Big as it was, it still didn't take long to scour the perimeter and find nothing more than a side pool where some type of mollusks clung to the rocks. Mica let go of Geoff's hand and stooped to pluck them off.

"Cook them I will," he said simply.

"Good idea. We need to keep our strength up, and the variety from the fish will be welcome."

He gazed up at the waterfall to see if it were possible to climb up and out. The walls were slick and therefore dangerous, but more, the opening from which light and water poured in was too narrow for either of them to squeeze through. If up was no good, then down it might have to be. He peered into the larger pool and couldn't see the bottom of it. That was not surprising. There had to be somewhere for the fish to come from and the water to drain. Geoff gnawed at his bottom lip as he considered the possibility of this being their only means of escape.

He turned to Mica. "Can you swim?"

The boy looked at him from the fire pit, where he had lit some more moss. "Swim?"

"Ah, of course not." *Not much call for that kind of skill in the desert.* "No matter." He scratched the back of his neck as he pondered some more the potential route out. Raised by a lake as he'd been, Geoff had played with his brothers under water his entire life, much to the worry of their mother. He was confident in his own skills, and there might be underwater channels short enough to allow Geoff to propel Mica through—assuming Mica could learn to hold his breath for a sufficient amount of time. There was no point in speculating, however. He'd have to have a look for himself.

He sat to strip off his boots, then stood to shed his pants. "I'm going to see what's under the water."

Mica already had the shellfish sizzling in the fire. "Why?"

"There may be useful information down there," was all he said. There was no point in causing Mica any alarm by speaking about something that might not be possible anyway.

The water was quite frigid, coming from the mountain top as it did. That was a wonderful temperature to slake one's thirst—not great for swimming, though. His dick shrank and his balls tried their best to climb into his body. Because he knew from experience that it was best to get it over with quickly, he hurried toward the center of the pool until his feet no longer touched the surface of the bottom. He ducked his head once to wet it while treading water. Then taking a deep breath, he dove under.

It wasn't as murky as he'd anticipated, and there were more denizens there than the fish they'd eaten.

The creatures scattered at his big intrusion into their calm domain. He was grateful for the room actually, as some of them slithered through the water rather than swam, and he wasn't sure if any of those aquatic snakes were poisonous. Better, he saw plants. If they were stuck in the cavern, meat and fish alone wouldn't sustain them forever. They'd need vegetation, although really if they didn't find a way out, the cave would become their tomb. Maybe it would be better to go quickly than languish for the gods knew how long for a rescue that would never come. It wasn't obvious to him that those on the outside even knew about the cave-in. They might not discover the problem until they returned for Mica's emergence. Then what? Could they clear the rocks? Maybe — or maybe they would assume the worst and not want to risk any more lives.

Geoff was a fast swimmer and good at holding his breath, so it didn't take more than a few dives for him to explore the entire pool. He found various places where the water flowed out and fish swam in. None of it was a path that a human could take. The openings weren't wide. It was part disappointment and part relief. It would be easier on Mica to explore a way through the mountain on foot. They could only hope there was a relatively convenient journey to the surface and that there were more caverns that could provide them with food and water. There was only so much they'd be able to carry out of this one.

* * * *

Mica rushed forward with handfuls of moss to rub down Geoff when he surfaced for good. "Freezing you are," he admonished. He didn't add that each time the man had disappeared beneath the water, Mica had been terrified he wouldn't surface again. Not that he worried the man would abandon him, but he didn't know what lurked down there. It might have been very dangerous. "To the fire come."

A shivering Geoff allowed Mica to propel him over and sit. The heat of the fire helped to warm him, so that by the time Mica had dried off all the water, the shaking had stopped.

"Thank you, darling. That water was very cold, indeed. Also, I'm afraid there is no hope of escaping that way."

Mica hid his relief, foolish as it was, and handed him some cooked mollusks that he'd removed from their shells. "Here. Tasty they are."

Geoff popped one into his mouth without hesitation. "Mmm. I agree. A bit fatty, as well. That's good. We need that for strength. Have you eaten?"

Mica nodded. "Yes." He rubbed his stomach. "An appetite I have not, though."

Geoff took Mica's chin between his forefinger and thumb, forcing Mica to look at him. "Eat some more. I know it's hard, given how difficult our situation is, but we must have courage and make ourselves as strong as possible for what is to come. I will do everything in my power to get you out of here." He let go and ate some more.

The man's words gave Mica heart. He didn't want false promises, and Geoff wasn't giving him any. He plucked a mollusk out of Geoff's hand. "A plan you have?"

Geoff inclined his head. "Of sorts. We must provision ourselves as best we can and return to the blocked cavern. We'll take the other tunnel and see where it leads us."

"Agreed." Mica had already assumed that and had given some thought to how they might carry water and food with them. They had little to accomplish that, but at least they had each other. It wasn't logical to feel that they had a chance because they were together. Geoff held no power to provide them with a safe exit if the mountain had none to give. Still, he believed they were stronger as a team, and that hope couldn't hurt.

They made short work of their meal. Then Mica set about catching and cooking more fish and mollusks to take with them. He and Geoff were both sacrificing their clothing to fashion bags to carry them and as much moss as they could. He'd unstrung the beads of his vest to use the string to tie bundles. His mother had made it for him, as mothers did for their sons, and it pained him to leave the precious, colored stones behind. There was no help for it, though. If something couldn't be drunk, eaten or used as fire, it had to be discarded. The pouch Mica had been provisioned with could function as a water skin. It wasn't very large, but it would have to do. Hopefully they'd find more water along the way — if not a pool, then at least dripping down the walls.

He was left with only his thong to wear, which didn't bother him, even though the cave was a bit chilly and the tunnels might be even more so. Geoff was entirely naked, except for his boots, something that did disturb Mica. Despite their predicament, he found it impossible to ignore the large, thick cock and heavy balls swinging between the man's legs. He'd felt it a few times now, indirectly. Seeing it was another thing entirely. The size of it should have alarmed him.

Instead, it aroused him so much that his dick was nearly bursting out of his thong. There was no way for him to hide it, and under the circumstances, it didn't seem necessary to be modest. They might never make it out alive. He understood that and was growing determined to make the most of the time they had.

As he approached Geoff, the man did a double take, his gaze fixing on Mica's bulge. A grin spread across his handsome face and his free dick rose up in greeting.

"Darling Mica, you make me forget what a serious predicament we're in."

Mica gave him what he hoped was an inviting look. "So bad is that? Sure I am no difference it will make if some pleasure we take before our journey we start." He paused and tried something he'd been intending to since Geoff had first agreed to the marriage. "We…might…not another chance have. Have another chance," he amended in a low voice, because that was a reality they had to face, and he was pleased to have spoken to Geoff in the manner he was used to successfully — mostly successful. It would take time to learn it properly, and he dearly prayed they would have it.

"Oh, my dear boy." Geoff reached for Mica's thong. "Sweet and clever you are."

Mica grinned at Geoff's returned effort. He stopped him, however, by gripping his wrist before he could touch Mica's dick. "Wait. My turn."

He didn't give Geoff a chance to agree. Using his hold, he pulled them together and grabbed Geoff's cock with his other hand. The shaft was heavy and warm, the skin soft as the finest leather. It pulsed within his hold as if a living thing separate from the man it was attached to. It was almost as if it was communicating.

Touch me. Lick me. Suck me. With a groan, Mica dropped to his knees and obeyed.

His first lick was tentative. He was unsure what to do. No one had ever instructed him in this manner of pleasuring, but he had seen a man do this to another once. It had been a guilty moment of spying on what should have been private. He conjured up the experience now to guide him through. The next lick was bolder. He ran this tongue up the shaft and around the head. Geoff's groan told him he was doing a good job. Emboldened, he lapped all around the dick with faster, surer strokes. He held the shaft at its bottom with one hand and let go of Geoff's wrist to cup the heavy balls with the other. He rolled the hidden globes within the sack because it seemed an obvious way to increase the experience for Geoff — and he enjoyed playing with them.

Then Mica let himself stop thinking and planning and just *did*, savoring the salty taste of the skin and the drops of cum bubbling up from the slit at the top. And because he wanted more, he opened his mouth wide and sucked the cockhead in. With another groan, Geoff gripped Mica's hair — not hard and he didn't try to control his movements. He was just functioning as an anchor for the man as he stood taking the pleasure Mica gave. There was only so much Mica could take in, but he made the most of it, working the shaft with his tongue where it sat, heavy and insistent.

The cock suddenly swelled, the only warning before cum flooded Mica's mouth. He swallowed hard, not wanting to waste a drop of it. A strange thought crossed his mind that he could live on Geoff's spending alone. He massaged the man's balls to milk them dry. And as he did so, his own orgasm caught him by surprise. The force of it sent him reeling forward, choking on Geoff's dick. He didn't go far, though, because Geoff had him, holding him in place until the last of his climax drained out of him.

* * * *

It seemed pointless to wear a cum-soaked thong or a wet one. Instead, after rinsing it in the pool, Mica had tied it around his thigh in case it came in handy later on. Their survival was dependent on what they already held. There could be no assurances that anything useful would be found elsewhere within the cave. And if Geoff was making the journey naked, so would he. There was nothing to hide between them now. They headed toward an unknown fate, Geoff in the lead, naturally. The man held the torch up high as they made their way through the unexplored tunnel. It was much like the other, although damper as they went farther in. That was all to the good. They lapped at water dripping down the walls to conserve what they carried. Neither of them said anything, yet they both knew this was a good sign. After lack of air, thirst was the next thing to fell a person. The tunnel wasn't stuffy enough to make them worried about the former, and of course, if they could breathe easily, it gave them hope that there were openings ahead of them. Maybe one would be human-sized.

Mica estimated that they'd been walking for many hours, resting only briefly, when they came across another cavern around a sharp bend. It wasn't as big as the other two and had no pool of water of any note. There was only a stagnant puddle below where water trickled down in earnest through a narrow crevice above. But there was also moss, which was a blessing, as the torch was nearly out. He quickly went about gathering some and forming a firepit. It wouldn't last long, though. He unpacked some of the food then portioned it out enough to mollify their stomachs while stretching their provisions. It was impossible to say how long it would take to find a way out. *If we ever do.* No, he couldn't think that way. Despair was the worst enemy they had at the moment.

As he and Geoff consumed their meager meal, something wiggling in the corner around a pile of dirt caught Mica's eye. Tossing the last of his ration into his mouth, Mica got up to investigate. He grinned at what he saw, and picking up one of the creatures, he showed it to Geoff. "Grubs. Edible they are."

Geoff made a face. "I've probably had worse on some of my campaigns, so I won't complain. Insects make for good food. It's surprising to find them down here and clever of you to spot it."

Warmed by the praise, Mica quickly gathered up as many of the grubs as he could find, then stoking the fire, he tossed them in. It was possible to eat them raw…but unappetizing. As long as they were able to safely make a fire, they should make use of it. When they were cooked and cooled, he stowed them away, banked what was left of the flames and sat down beside Geoff.

"Come here." Geoff gathered Mica in his arms and laid them down so that Mica's head was on his chest.

Despite their tiredness and hunger, they both hardened quickly. Hands and mouths made for great pleasure, but Mica dared to press for what he really wanted. "Fuck me will you? Please?"

"No. This is not the time or place, I'm afraid," he added before Mica could raise an objection. "I don't want to hurt you. Best to wait until we are properly wed and I have access to oil to ease the way. You can't imagine how painful taking my cock would be without some help."

Tears threatened to spill over. He worked to get the words in his head out right. "I do not wish to as a virgin die." He shook his head in frustration. "Die as a virgin."

Geoff briefly squeezed him so hard Mica gasped. "You won't. I swear I won't let that happen. In the meantime..." He flipped Mica onto his side and spooned him from behind.

The man's long, thick cock slid between Mica's ass cheeks, the length of him brushing against Mica's hole, a maddening tease of what could be. It wasn't what he wanted, but it was better than anything he'd experienced so far. The rubbing across his hole sent a warmth into his ass. He moaned and pressed back at the thrusting. Geoff clasped Mica's dick with his large hand, easily encasing the shaft in his hold. A few jerks and Mica was convulsing with his orgasm. A splash of wet against his crack and a loud groan reverberated through the cavern. When they were finished, they lay quietly entwined.

Mica should have been exhausted, and he *was* tired. But he also didn't want to waste the little time that they might have without knowing more about this man whom he was falling in love with. Much of what Geoff had told him that first night together in the desert had been impersonal. He wanted more. *Love him I do.* Perhaps it was their facing death that forced the issue to his mind. He wasn't ready to say the words out loud. He wouldn't hold back, however, if their situation became obviously dire. He couldn't die without revealing what was in his heart.

"Of your family tell me."

"Hmm? Oh, well there's not much to it. My parents are landed nobility of a minor status, although we live a very comfortable life. I'm the youngest of five sons."

"No sisters have you?"

There was a brief tightening of Geoff's hold and in his voice. "My parents had a daughter born after me. I can picture her a little, all soft curls and frilly dresses. She died before she reached two years, a fever that took a lot of people one winter. I remember the pall of grief that descended in our lives for a long while. My mother in particular was devastated. She still ran the household as usual and participated in family meals and celebrations, but there was a hollowness to her that faded only after I'd was much older. The gods have been kind to her, though, in recent years. Those of my brothers who are married have fathered only girls, as the gods would have it. There's a gaggle of them running around the manor at any given time. It's a comfort to her."

Mica ran his fingers over Geoff's hand. "Babies my mother lost, too, after me. A joy my brother Lye is, though. The son of my father's dreams he is."

Geoff rubbed his chin along the top of Mica's head. "Now, you can't tell me your father doesn't appreciate you."

Mica couldn't hold back the sigh. "A disappointment I am. Not a warrior, but a stable hand."

"There's nothing wrong with tending to horses. They are crucial to your People, I'm sure. You should be proud of your skills, even if they aren't in warfare."

Mica chuckled. "Says the warrior."

"Well, yes *I'm* suited to the life of a soldier. That's just me. Not that I had much choice. I was son number five, after all."

"What matters that?"

"Among my people, it's pretty standard for children's lots in life to be based on birth order. My oldest brother will inherit the family estate, so had to master working the land and managing the people who live and labor there. My second brother is the diplomat of the family. He serves the king while recommending policy that can advantage us in some way. Not that the king is easily swayed to favor one type of subject over another, but it is the way of my country and many others I have visited to strive for benefits."

"Here as well. Whispers in the ears of the chief and shaman are made."

"And those two are your family. I suppose that makes you a member of the ruling class here and by extension of our marriage, me as well."

Mica curled his fingers around Geoff's arm. "Matters to you?" He felt a pang of disappointment, which was ridiculous. Geoff was already influenced in his desire for Mica by the fact that Mica had saved his life. The man was beholding to him for that fact alone. The idea that he might find satisfaction in gaining prominence by marrying Mica was beside the point. This was no love match—for Geoff anyway. Mica's impulsive offer to invoke the ancient offer of marriage had always been based on a strong personal desire that likely had been the precursor to love.

Geoff's hold tightened briefly. "Only to the extent that it means I can barter some kind of treaty with your chief."

"Treaty?"

"An exchange of promises that mutually benefit both countries. Is that not something you do here?"

"I know not. Trading we do, sometimes. The same it is?"

"Yes, actually. That's as a succinct a definition of what a treaty means as any. We could use provisions for the next leg of our journey, and I'm hoping your chief will be willing to supply some in exchange for…well, I'm not actually sure what. I can only promise future dealings between our people in the vaguest of ways, given that I will not be returning to Moorcondia for a long time."

Because the reminder of how he'd be tied to this man and his wanderings for the rest of his life and might never see his family again saddened him, Mica turned the talk back to more pleasant things. "Your other brothers do what?"

Geoff stroked Mica's arm. "Ah yes. The third brother was sent to serve the gods at the local monastery."

"Understand I do not." It was true but he also liked the sound of Geoff's voice. It was comforting in the growing darkness of the cavern and despite his fatigue wanted to keep the talk going.

"It's like being a shaman, sort of."

"Oh." That struck him as odd. Among the People, only women were able to commune with the Earth Mother. Then again, it was obvious that Geoff's people had different ideas about who governed the world. Not wanting to get into that topic, he kept it to the personal still. "Pray he does all day?" It seemed impossible for someone to do only that.

"I'm sure he does, although his order is well-known for making excellent ale, a type of drink," he clarified. "They sell it to sustain their prayerful way of life."

"And the other?"

"The last of my older brothers married into the largest textiles family in all of Moorcondia. They buy all the wool we shear from our sheep, a kind of wooly animal, so it was quite the successful union as far as our families are concerned. He is by far the richest of us and growing fat and happy as a husband and father."

"Helping family, important it is." The more he learned about Geoff's homeland, the happier he was to realize his new life wouldn't be that different from the one he knew.

Geoff yawned loudly. "Then there is me, the soldier. I could have chosen something else, I suppose, although I can't imagine what. Honestly, it's a good fit for me. I like being outside and active. War is horror, though, and one I have little stomach for now I'm older. I'm glad to have this exploration mission to fill the next few years to come. I can fight if needed yet hope to avoid it. Obviously my decisions recently are not a good indication of my judgment."

Mica snuggled closer and yawned himself. He couldn't keep his eyes open any more. "Glad I am that they were not."

He drifted off with the sound of Geoff's chuckling in his ear.

* * * *

Geoff held the blackened stub of the torch as high as possible to cast light on their path. The heat from it was enough to irritate the skin on his finger, yet the last of the moss and the rope binding it to the wooden handle were nearly spent. Soon they would be plunged into darkness. They would have to depend on touch alone to navigate the mountain tunnels. It would be even slower going, and they risked tumbling into a crevasse if they weren't careful. *Or even if we are.* Both he and Mica were hungry, tired, dirty and afraid that their fate was to be buried in this mountain. At least that was his fear. He didn't speak of it because Mica was depending on his being strong for them both — not that the boy had been anything other than resourceful and stoic. Still, it must remind him of being trapped in the quicksand with no way out unless someone intervened to save him.

That someone had been Geoff before, and it would be him again. He was determined to get them out of this damnable place so that he could marry the boy and take care of him for the rest of their lives. There simply *had* to be a way out. Mountain caves and tunnels were forged over eons by water. He knew that because he'd paid some attention to his lessons as a boy. And the water trickling along the walls in various places confirmed the truth. If there was a way in for the water, there had to be a way out for them.

They came to a fork, an uncommon occurrence thus far. As he showed the light down each passageway, he saw that the ground to the left appeared to slope up. He'd thought they'd been ascending for some time. It had been a gradual change, so he couldn't be sure of his perception. This time he could tell it was true from the obvious tilt of the floor. With a renewed sense of purpose, he guided Mica in that direction. After a while, the tunnel walls widened in a sure sign that they were approaching a cavern. Before they entered it, the torch sputtered and died for good. He stumbled to a halt, trying to gain his bearings before continuing in the dark. Beside him Mica clutched at his hand, the boy's breathing loud and harsh.

Geoff took a tentative step forward, blinking his eyes in the vain hope of seeing something — anything. Clutching the charred wood, he placed that hand against the wall as a guide. Edging forward, he continued to walk. Then the wall curved and he had to stop once more as the passageway opened up. He smelled the fresher air before he saw their salvation. Across the gloom there was a beam of light.

Chapter Seven

Geoff placed Mica onto a relatively flat rock. "Wait here while I see what's beyond this."

The boy acquiesced without question, although he radiated unmistakable excitement. *Of course he did.* The desert-dweller had good skills and instincts, despite not being suited as a warrior. He didn't need to be told that where there was light, there was a way to the surface. The only question was whether it was large enough for them to wiggle through.

But there was no point in worrying what might be. With his sight adjusted, Geoff was able to pick his way around the uneven ground littered with stalagmites. There was no water pooled here, only rock and sand. On the far side, where the shaft of light came from, another narrow passage sloped up. Other than the way they'd come in, it was the only way out again, and he feared that if this wasn't a path up to the surface, they'd be forced to backtrack and try their luck with the other way. He didn't like that idea, because that ground hadn't gone up at all and might even lead downward, farther into the belly of the mountain.

As he scrambled up, however, he couldn't hold back a grin as his surroundings grew brighter and the source of the sunlight proved to be a decent-sized opening. He pulled himself onto a ledge and stuck his face into the opening. It didn't matter that the day was waning. He could see the sky, and that meant they were nearly free. He tested the rock surrounding the fissure and found it loose. Carefully, he tugged one free and sent it scattering down. Then he tried another. Pebbles and dirt rained down on him, so he stopped, not daring to breathe, worried he was going to cause a collapse. When nothing more happened, he cautiously continued. Soon the opening was sufficiently big for him to stick his head out. He closed his eyes as he took a deep, cleansing breath.

"Geoff?"

He ducked down again to see Mica standing at the bottom of the slope, a look of hope on his face. "Careful, darling. More rock will fall while I widen this hole."

"A way out, it is?"

Geoff dared to smile broadly. "It is. We just need to create more space to get through." He didn't add that he thought it likely he'd only be able to make it big enough for Mica. His own broad shoulders would need more room than he believed was possible.

Stop borrowing trouble.

"Stand back."

Once Mica complied, Geoff got on with the work of removing all the loose rock he could put his hands on. By the time he was finished, he was coated in more grime than ever, and he wheezed from the clouds of dirt he sent up. But it would do.

He carefully descended to where Mica waited. "Come on, darling. Time to get you out."

Mica didn't say anything or move a muscle until he suddenly threw his arms around Geoff and held on tight for long seconds. Although he made no sound, it was obvious the boy was crying. Geoff gave him the time he needed to pull himself together and let go.

Geoff guided Mica to go first, up the slope and to squeeze into the spot right below the opening. "Out you go. Free your hands first, then your head. I'll boost the rest of you through."

Tired as he was, the fact that he had his hands firmly on this beautiful boy's backside caused no stirring in Geoff's cock. That would change, though. Soon they would be married, and his dick would get as much action as Mica was willing to give it. But that was the future. All he felt now was elation as he pushed Mica up and out, the last bit done by hugging his legs and shoving.

Mica disappeared for a second, then his face showed through the opening. He was smiling broadly, and tears clearly showed on his cheeks. "Get you out now, I will. Go down."

Scanning the perimeter of the hole, Geoff grimaced. "I don't think any more of it can be dislodged. Go back to your people for help. They may be able to find another way out for me."

"No!" Mica's tone was fierce, unlike any he'd used before. "I. Will. Get. You. Out." He thrust the words past his lips with both obvious difficulty...and determination.

Geoff couldn't help but be proud of the boy. And although he worried that it was a futile effort that might do more harm than good to the exit, he had to give the boy a chance to succeed, so he did as he'd been told. He walked all the way down to the bottom of the slope and sheltered himself beside an edge of rock. Not only did Mica deserve the chance to try, but being on the surface perhaps gave him a better vantage point than Geoff to see the potential for success.

Mica disappeared for a while. Then the end of a stout branch stuck through the opening. It was leveraged against the rock on one side, and it was obvious that Mica was using it to dislodge that which couldn't be moved with only one's hands. There was grunting and a shower of fine rocks and dirt. Then a cascade of the same headed toward Geoff. He rushed back into the cavern to avoid it, coughing against the cloud of dust. When it was quiet again, he gave himself a moment to grieve his loss of freedom and console himself with the fact that Mica was out and…safe?

He rushed back to the passageway. "Mica!"

Through the remaining debris swirling about, light bathed him. A hand waved to him from the large opening that now existed at the top of the slope.

"Come, Geoff."

Geoff didn't have to be told twice. He scrambled up and through the sharp rocks, not minding the pain to his hands, arms and legs, and clasped the offered hand. He let Mica help him through and out and knelt on the ground above.

Raising his face to the setting sun, he said, "Thank the gods. Thank *you*," he added, grabbing Mica into a tight hug.

Now the boy gave way entirely to his emotions, a flood of tears splashed against Geoff's skin and the sound of sobs squeezed his heart. His own eyes pricked a bit, as well, but he concentrated on giving his darling boy the comfort he needed. What they'd been through would scare anyone, even a hardened soldier such as himself. That someone as sweet as Mica had survived the ordeal with such courage was amazing, and this show of relief was nothing for him to be ashamed about.

"Kill you I thought I had," the boy said through staccato breath.

"Not at all, my dear. That small shower of rock was nothing that could harm me."

Mica pulled back and blinked his moist eyes at him. "No. Not that." He visibly swallowed hard. "Chose you I did for the initiation. Put you in that cave, I did."

"Ah." Geoff held back the smile that threatened to come out. Mica had seriously been holding in this guilt. It was up to him to set it free. "None of this was your fault. Even if you hadn't asked for me to be your guide, I was never going to sit by and let that asshole go with you." He frowned. "Lonan, is it?" When Mica nodded, Geoff grimaced. "Yes, he was not to be trusted."

He kissed Mica gently and briefly. Neither of them was up for more than a quick show of affection. "Nothing would have kept me from your side, and I would have chosen to be nowhere other than with you through his ordeal. No more guilt, understand?" He looked sternly at the boy.

Mica nodded.

"Good. Now come on. Let's find our way back to your village."

They stood with arms around each other's waists. Despite the difference in their sizes and physical strength, Geoff couldn't honestly say that he was the one supporting the boy so much as they kept each other upright and moving. Around an outcrop of rock, the view before them was heartwarming. The village could be seen — distant to be sure, yet not so far away that they couldn't make it in relatively short time, even taking into account how they'd have to navigate rocky terrain on more downward paths. This was not the plateau on which they planted their crops. This was a wild, uncultivated part of the mountain. He doubted anyone had ever been up here before them.

"All those passages took us around and up, but not so deep into the mountain." He looked down at Mica's shining face. "Do you think you can make it home—or should I go get help." There was nothing more than an overhang to shield Mica from the sun, but then again, night was falling and being the desert, the temperature would drop significantly. A naked Mica would get cold—perhaps dangerously so.

Besides all that, he wasn't sure he could let go of the boy at this point.

Mica made the decision easy. "Go with you I will."

"All right." He licked his dry lips. They'd finished their water not so long ago, and while the inside of the mountain had provided some at decent intervals, he doubted the outside was any more accommodating on that point than the desert was. But such gloomy expectations had been obliterated by their escape, so he would stay positive for his own sake as much as for Mica. "Maybe we'll find some water along the way."

* * * *

The Earth Mother and her child, the mountain, were kind to them. There was a small trickle of water to be found on their way down to the village. It wasn't much and it was warm, but Mica licked what he could with gratitude. And there were more grubs wiggling about and brush to use for a fire to cook them. Everything Mica knew about survival continued to allow him to help them on the last leg of their journey. Geoff undoubtedly could have done it all himself, yet he stood aside and let Mica contribute in the way he could. It took the man effort to give way, it was obvious to Mica. He knew Geoff well by now — his expressions, the way he held his body, the things he didn't say with his tongue but with his eyes. He was deliberately giving Mica free rein, and the confidence in Mica that it demonstrated only served to make the burgeoning love in Mica's heart grow.

As they sat, exhausted and pressed together to ward off the chill of the night, he wanted to reveal his feelings, yet couldn't quite get out the words. With their ordeal not over, he feared Geoff would dismiss any declarations of love as being driven by gratitude for surviving their circumstances and not genuine affection. *Our first night together after we wed, tell him I will.* That was a sensible plan and wouldn't require him to bite his tongue for too much longer.

Geoff didn't allow them to linger long. He had them up and moving again shortly after they finished their meager meal. It became easier to keep going by focusing on the sight of the village growing closer. To get there, however, required going down the mountain again. Paths were easy to find but tricky to navigate. Geoff held onto his hand tightly, always a step ahead to catch him if he slipped. It was such a sweet gesture. Mica didn't have the heart to tell the man that being raised a cave-dweller, he was as sure-footed as a goat. Geoff obviously liked being his protector, and besides, Mica loved having any reason for them to touch.

As they made their way down what Mica believed would be the last cliff before reaching the one that held the cave entrance, the sight of the village was gone, but a sound caught his ears.

Mica dug his heels in, forcing Geoff to stop as well. "Listen." He didn't know whether to be happy or sad. The chanting was the mourning of the People for one they had lost. To hear the sound so clearly meant his family and others had gathered at the mouth of the cave to lament his passing. He wanted to end the pain in those lamentations. "Faster, please."

Geoff seemed to understand. With a nod, he started them on their way again, a little faster this time, although they couldn't afford to risk their necks at this point. They were almost home free. But when they reached the flat ground, Mica couldn't stop himself. He took off as fast as his fatigue would allow him, tugging Geoff in his wake. When they rounded the side, he came to an abrupt stop, uncertain of how to intrude on the solemn ceremony before them.

His mother stood by the mouth of the cave, surrounded first by his father, who was holding Lye, and his sister, then the chief and other elders of the People. Virtually all the village spread out before them. Everyone was dressed in mourning red and responded to his mother's chants as tradition required. For some reason, it surprised him that so many mourned what he assumed was his passing. He hadn't thought he mattered much to anyone.

Geoff pressed against his side. "You should go to them now. It will be a shock — but a happy one."

Swallowing past a lump in his throat, Mica started forward. Except this time, he walked. It didn't take long before there was an audible gasp. Then another. Almost as one, the People turned in his direction and the chanting stopped. As he approached the outer part of the gathering, villagers parted. Everyone's eyes were wide, and a few mouths were hanging open. The scrutiny unnerved him, but he kept going until with a loud cry, his mother flew into him. The force of the hug she gave caused him to stumble back, and he lost his grip on Geoff's hand. There was nothing to be done about it, however, because his father joined them. They, along with a squealing Lye and a crying Alyn, held him captured within their embraces. He had never felt so loved...and yet he wiggled past them enough to grab Geoff's hand again and add him to the group. Surprisingly, his family didn't protest.

It was his mother, always the strongest of them all, who broke up the communal hug. She swiped away at the rare tears sliding down her cheeks. "Dead we thought you were."

"The cave-in we heard," his father said. "Dig you out we tried...and failed."

Mica heard the self-castigation in his father's voice. "Tried we as well on the other side. Impossible it was."

His father nodded and held on tightly to Lye when he tried to lean into Mica's arms. Then he looked at Geoff. "Saved my son you did. A good choice in guide you were after all."

"Thank you, sir, but you have to know that Mica did his part and then some. He used all the warriors' skills you taught him—finding us fuel for fire and food to cook in it. It would have been hard for me to escape my fate without him."

Mica's father turned his attention back to him. For the first time in his life, he saw pride in his eyes. He wasn't sure how he felt about having to overcome death in order to earn it.

"A man you are now."

The chief pushed his way to stand beside Mica's mother. "Celebrate we will both your manhood and your return. Thanks to the Earth Mother we must give."

Whooping erupted around them with the warriors ululating as if they'd just returned from a successful fight. As the noise died down, everyone started to head back to the village. Mica's father took off his red mourning robe and handed it over to him. "Clothes you need."

"And a bath," Alyn added with a grin and wrinkle of her nose.

So caught up in the drama of his own return from the dead, Mica had forgotten his and Geoff's physical state. They were not only naked but filthy — and probably smelling of cum as much as anything else. His cheeks warmed at the thought. He quickly wrapped the cloth around his waist and was both astounded and grateful when his sister gave her robe to Geoff.

With a wink, the man covered himself much the same way, although the cloth barely reached his mid-thigh. They really should have switched, but no sooner did he have that thought, than he was swept up by his family to leave the mountain and return home.

* * * *

"A virgin you are still?"

Mica gasped at his sister. "Such a question that is!" He smoothed his kilt and made sure his beaded vest was straight. Having his manhood celebration and getting married in the same night was nerve-racking.

Alyn finished with the braid she was putting in his hair and leaned against the wall with crossed arms. "Deny it you have not."

Mica tossed his head. "Yes. Careful with me Geoff was." *Too careful.* Given that they'd been separated the night they'd returned and he'd only glimpsed the man from afar the following two days, he was past ready to be properly bedded. If they'd gotten the deflowering done in the cave, he wouldn't be anxious about it. He wasn't worried that it would hurt—not more than necessary the first time. It was more a matter of not being able to please his husband as much as he knew the man would him.

Alyn straightened. "Good that is. Warmed to him Father has but suspicious he remains, too. Assure him I will."

Mica didn't have a chance to tell his sister that his virginity was not a subject he wanted to be bantered between his family members. The arrival of his parents to take him to the celebration made it impossible to talk further. It was pointless anyway. The marriage was imminent, so what difference did it make? He needed to concentrate on what he was about to do and forget what had happened in that cave.

Celebrations marking adulthood as well as marriages were occasions for the entire village to gather and feast. This time, he wasn't surprised to see everyone, or unnerved as they parted to let his family walk through to the chief's dais. Better, Geoff was standing there at the head of the crowd, wearing a warrior's kilt of dark leather threaded with beads and a matching vest. His feet were encased in the same low, soft boots as Mica's instead of the ones he'd rode in with. His hair was too short to be braided, but the bristles that had grown on his face while they were trapped had been scraped off. He was so handsome and imposing that Mica's heart stuttered and heat pooled in his groin. Having recovered from thirst, hunger and tiredness, Mica had no trouble getting hard. Only his thong kept it in check, but the tingling feel of his arousal made him impatient for the evening to end.

Wishful thinking. The People were big on ceremony, and the impending two different ones back-to-back would last well after the moon rose in the sky. He could do nothing more than flash a smile at Geoff before ascending the dais to accept his new position as an adult of the village and the wife of a warrior.

* * * *

Geoff had once more burst with pride seeing Mica being ushered into manhood. Despite the boy's concern that he wasn't warrior-like, he was treated as if he were. The chief and his father had presented him with a new knife, kilt and bow. They were large weapons, meant for fighting, and even though everyone there knew Mica was unlikely to use them for such, no one had smirked behind their hands or snickered. He had been treated with dignity and acted accordingly. He'd accepted the tokens of his manhood with seriousness and grace. And if his gaze had flitted toward Geoff now and again…? Well, that was all to the good, because the next ceremony of the evening was starting now.

Geoff and Mica stood side-by-side on the dais. Geoff wanted to hold Mica's hand in the Moorcondian way, but no one had indicated that was appropriate, so he kept his hands to himself and tried to follow what was happening. It was impossible. The shaman was in charge of this event, and she spoke rapidly with floral and convoluted metaphors and a lot of incantations to their deity — the Earth Mother. It was not unlike what he'd heard all his life from the priestly class. He took all belief with a grain of salt, so the words didn't matter to him. What was important was that he was that much closer to claiming Mica as his own, and his almost-wife seemed to take the procedure to heart. More than once, the boy's breath hitched and he blinked back tears—of joy, he hoped.

Of course they are. The little minx has been very clear on what he wants. And what he appeared to want was Geoff, which was all to the good, given that he wanted Mica as well. In fact, he'd never desired anything as much in his whole life. He'd been going slightly mad during his two-day recovery, not being able to speak to him, let alone hold him. That was all going to change shortly. He just had to be patient. Yet, as he stood there, all he could do was picture Mica in his arms, lying beneath him as he claimed the boy's body. He absolutely hated the way the thong he'd been given cramped his cock and balls and rode up his crack. At the moment, though, he understood the need for it. Otherwise, his kilt would be tented with his erection for all to see. The men of the People weren't so stupid as to make such obvious shows to their women.

The shaman went suddenly silent, forcing his focus back on her. She then presented a cup to Mica. He took a sip and handed it over to Geoff, his gaze cast downward in an adorable show of shyness. Understanding his role, Geoff accepted the cup and drained what little of the drink that was left. It was some kind of fermented fruit, too heavy to be called wine, and with a kick that burned all the way down his throat. He tried not to wince and handed the empty cup back to the shaman.

The woman spoke more words, then the crowd erupted in a cheer. Geoff understood that to mean the wedding was over, but that thought had barely crossed his mind before Mica pressed against him and raised his lips for a kiss. Geoff didn't need further prompting. He closed his mouth over his now-wife's and slipped his tongue inside. He tasted the alcohol first.

Underneath that was the unique sweetness that was Mica. Perhaps it wasn't good form to ravage the boy like this in front of everyone. He couldn't help himself, and Mica didn't try to escape him. If anything, he clung to him more and kissed him back with the same amount of passion.

It was everyone else who forced them apart. With whoops and hollers, they were separated by various hands, being gently shoved through the crowd until they landed on a large blanket among a sea of such coverings laid out in the center of the village. Mica's family soon joined them. Food and drink were passed around. There was a storm of activity until everyone was sitting down on their respective blankets based on family, he had to assume, and the meal began.

Geoff had gorged himself since coming out of the cave to make up for the hunger he'd experienced. He assumed it had been the same for Mica. Still, he was hungry once more and intended to eat just enough to satisfy his stomach but not so much as to weigh him down for the night's coming activities. First, though, he had to make sure that his wife was cared for. *My wife.* That was going to take some getting used to—and not only because his wife was a boy. He'd never intended to marry. That term was for other men, not him. Yet here he was, and try as he might, he couldn't summon any regrets. Mica was the right person for him, even though their circumstances were as bizarre as they came. Geoff couldn't shake the feeling that his entire life had been leading him to Mica, who by his own admission had been dreaming of him.

Is this truly love? He had to face his unfamiliar sensations once more. *No, that can't be.* He wasn't prone to sentiment of that kind. Of course he loved his family, but the idea of someone capturing his heart boggled his mind. His brother George had once told him that he would have taken his merchant wife if she'd come to him barefoot and in her slip. He loved her, not her family's wealth and status, not the economic benefit it brought to his family. One look at her and he'd fallen hard, or so he said, and the rest was merely icing on the cake. Geoff had dismissed the confession at the time because George had always been a dreamer. Looking at Mica, however, made him realize that George had the right of it all along. Geoff wanted Mica, not only the pleasure that the boy would bring him in bed.

As he held out a piece of bread to his bride, his stomach dropped from the boy's smile of gratitude. He was trapped deep, it seemed, and, unlike with the mountain, he had no wish to escape.

Chapter Eight

Mica waved Geoff into the cave dwelling. "This night, here all newlyweds spend. Not much."

Sensing his wife was feeling insecure and obviously nervous, Geoff hurried to reassure him. Glancing around the small space dominated by a simple pallet, he pulled Mica into an embrace. "It's perfect, darling."

He meant it. The spot was at the far end of the village, giving them more privacy than most. He wasn't planning on shouting out his pleasure, but he did intend to coax some amount of noise out of his bride. He walked them over to the pallet and helped Mica to sit on it. The bedding was clean and smelled like fresh flowers, even though there weren't any inside the cave. As he knelt to take off Mica's boots, he took in more detail of their surroundings. There was a low rock acting as a table and on it sat a jug of what he assumed was water or more fermented drink, a plate of bread and dried fruit, and a small bowl filled with some kind of cream. That had been his request, made to the older man – the stable master – who'd tended to him while he recovered and had prepared him for the marriage. Noshi, as he'd introduced himself, hadn't batted an eye. If anything, his expression implied that the request pleased him.

Mica began to remove his vest. Geoff stayed his hand. "Let me. I want to unwrap you myself — as an after-dinner treat."

A rosy-red stained the boy's cheeks. "All of me you have seen already. No surprises are there left."

Geoff slid his hand up one thigh. "I haven't had the pleasure of watching you like this, lying on a soft bed for the taking as I strip you. This is the first time I'm going to see my wife and not merely my lover, and that's special, too."

Mica's lips parted on a sigh, and he raised his eyes, showing blown pupils and a scorching heat of need. The sight of it nearly made Geoff come before they'd barely begun to make love. He gritted his teeth and concentrated on the task at hand. Mica permitted Geoff to handle him the way a girl might do a doll. He rolled the boy this way and that, peeling off the vest and untying the kilt. Mica's beautiful body revealed itself bit by bit, and yes, seeing him now was something new. He could look at his wife — really look. He could take his time to explore every inch with both his gaze and his hands.

Geoff did so, leaving only the thong in place, Mica's cock making it bulge and the tip of his dick peeking out from the top. But that was the end point. No need to rush matters. They'd both benefit from the waiting. So he started at the top, leaning over his wife and kissing him. At the same time, he stroked the boy's arms, playing his fingers along the skin. Mica shivered at the touch and moaned. Geoff swallowed the sound and deepened the kiss, sweeping his tongue around every part of his bride's mouth. As usual, Mica didn't remain passive. He met Geoff at each point, wrestling his tongue with his own.

Now they both moaned. Geoff's arms began to shake, more from having to control his mounting desire than muscle fatigue. Nevertheless, he lowered himself down on one elbow next to Mica and continued his gentle assault on the boy's body by planting kisses along his jaw. He kept his free hand busy by roaming it across Mica's chest, pausing to twirl each nipple between his thumb and forefinger. His bride rewarded him with panting breath and shuddering against his hold. There was nothing for it but to press his lips down the boy's throat and onto his pecs before taking one of the buds raised by his fingers into his mouth. He sucked hard on each one in turn and even scraped his teeth against the dusky skin around them.

Mica writhed and clutched at Geoff's arm. "Please."

Geoff let go to ask, "Please what?" He knew the answer, of course. It was perhaps mean of him to tease his wife so, but he couldn't help himself. He'd never been with someone as naked in what he wanted and needed than this virginal boy.

"Please, more." Now Mica whimpered and bucked his hips.

The invitation was clear. Still, Geoff didn't rush. He lapped his way down the boy's flat, firm belly until his mouth hit the top of the thong. There was a little taste of cum where Mica's cock had managed to escape its confines. Geoff licked it greedily.

"Hmm. You taste marvelous. I want more."

He slid down to where he'd always intended to end up. Using his teeth, he tugged the thong away while releasing the string holding it in place. As soon as the dick sprang free, he sucked it down to the root. Mica's small, slender cock was an easy morsel and tasted both sweet and salty. Geoff swallowed around it and worked it with his tongue. Mica came within seconds, convulsing as if he'd never come from Geoff's ministrations before. It made him sorry he hadn't reciprocated the blow job earlier. Geoff held on until the trembling stopped. He slowly pulled away, licking the cock clean before he let it go.

For a few seconds, he simply sat back on his haunches and stared at the beautiful boy lying in front of him—thoroughly debauched and obviously spent. His lips were still wet and puffy from Geoff's kisses, and color bloomed across his face and chest. Geoff was ridiculously pleased to see he'd left marks on his wife to evidence his successful efforts.

Just when it appeared as if Mica had fallen asleep, he opened his eyes. "Fuck me you will."

It was a command more than a question. Geoff didn't hesitate to comply. Perhaps a more considerate husband would urge his wife to rest a bit. He couldn't wait, though. His need to mount the boy was nearly overwhelming. And it would take some time still to get there, more than his bride would probably like. But care had to be taken. He wasn't going to hurt his wife any more than could be helped. He began to strip off his own clothing as he went to fetch the cream. He was careful removing the clothing Mica's father had gifted him with, yet wasted no time getting naked. He folded his kilt and laid it and the vest on top of Mica's. Then he set his boots beside his wife's and took a second to admire how right it looked for them to be together like that, how symbolic of their union it was.

Geoff turned to present his hard cock for Mica's inspection. "I want to give this to you now, darling. It's time."

Mica nodded. "Yes."

"We must both be patient, however. I want to do this exactly right."

The one problem was that Geoff had never lain with a virgin before. He understood basically what needed to be done but was also determined to take the most conservative route to breaching his wife. He put down the bowl and reached for Mica to flip him over. The boy once again let him do whatever he wanted with his body.

"Let's get you kneeling." Although he would have preferred to look at Mica's lovely face while thrusting into him, he believed he'd have more control over his movements this way. He raised Mica's ass with his legs spread and made sure he was braced against both forearms.

"Comfortable?"

"Yes." The boy's voice was already thick with passion.

In this position, Mica's hole was on full display. The dusky puckered ring called to Geoff. He wet a finger and swirled it around, not trying to penetrate. The hole spasmed, and Mica gave a breathy moan. *No surprise there.* It was an erotic spot on one's body as well as a functional one. He had no idea why, but one could see a design of the gods in it. Hands and mouths were excellent ways to give one another pleasure, yet there was nothing quite like sinking his cock into this tight hole. And from what his lovers had conveyed, there was just as much to enjoy on the receiving end.

Because there was a fine line between caution and torture, he wasted no more time coating that same finger with cream. When he returned, he pressed it inside. He'd expected resistance. Instead, Mica welcomed the finger with ease. Geoff slid it in as far as it could go and wiggled it around to press against Mica's prostate. The low groan and the way the hole gripped his finger told Geoff he'd hit his mark. He pulled back, then thrust, repeating the movement until he was fucking Mica's ass with his finger. It didn't take long for his wife to push back against the invasion, a clear invitation for more. So, he added a second finger to pry the channel open. He could feel when both the ring and the passage loosened even more.

From his vantage point, he could see how tight Mica's balls were, pressed against his body. The boy was obviously and not surprisingly hard again. Geoff's own dick was howling with the need to be driven into Mica's ass, and his balls ached as if they'd been kicked. *Too bad.* They'd have to wait. His wants hardly mattered compared to his wife's. He might not have been looking for this in his life, but he was damn sure going to do right by this boy.

When he judged it was time to increase the pressure, he added a third finger. Now it was harder to breach Mica's hole. There was more resistance, and a hitching of the boy's breath that told him he was in some discomfort. Geoff held his fingers in place and lay his free palm on the small of his wife's back. He made lazy circles to help him relax.

"Such a beautiful boy you are. That's it, easy now."

"All right I am," Mica panted. "More I want."

"When you've relaxed again." Geoff continued to caress the boy's back while holding his fingers still. He would stay this way the rest of the night, if need be. He gave the same advice as his weapons trainer had to help him calm himself. "Deep breaths, darling. In and out. That's it. Slowly."

Once Mica's hole loosened again, Geoff returned to thrusting. He kept his movements slow and steady, allowing Mica's ass to get used to being stretched.

Mica cried out and convulsed, his channel gripping Geoff's fingers. He didn't need to look or be told that his wife had come again from the finger fucking alone. As the boy panted through his climax, Geoff judged it time. He pulled out his fingers and grabbed a handful of cream. He slathered it all over his dick while positioning himself closer to Mica's backside. The hole still spasmed, so he wasted no time pressing the head of his cock past the ring. There was resistance again, but not as much, and it was gone in an instant. He gripped Mica by the hips and pulled him back as he pushed forward until he was balls deep. His dick was encased in warm grip that made him groan, loud and long.

It hurt. Mica had known it would, yet it was more of an overwhelming sense of fullness than true pain. With his eyes closed and his heart still racing from his last climax, he forced himself to take deep, steady breaths and relax—just as his husband had taught him. And it worked as it had earlier to loosen his sphincter. He was glad it was becoming easier to take Geoff's cock, not that he would have stopped him if it hadn't. His husband had given him so much pleasure already. He reveled in the idea that it was his turn to make the man's eyes cross and his heart stop. Judging by the sounds Geoff was making, Mica was succeeding very well indeed. When Geoff had managed to stick his dick all the way inside, he'd stopped and simply held Mica's ass against his groin. He continued to do so in a remarkable show of control, and Mica appreciated the extra time to acclimate to the invasion. It was obvious, however, from the slight trembling of his husband that the man's limits were being tested.

And because he wanted them both to experience the most they could from the mounting, Mica wiggled his hips and tried to buck backward in invitation. His message was received. Geoff pulled his cock out slowly almost completely before sliding it back in again. They both moaned that time. Then the man began to thrust in earnest, picking up speed with each pass until he was fucking Mica hard and fast. Mica became aroused again and once more convulsed with a third orgasm. At nearly the same moment, warmth splashed inside him and bathed his channel. His husband let out a growl and tightened his grip on Mica's hips. He smacked against Mica's ass a few more times before collapsing beside him. Mica started to collapse on his belly. Geoff caught him as he fell and held him tightly against him before Mica landed.

"Did I hurt you?"

Mica smiled against his chest. "Kill me you did. Do it again, will you?"

On a laugh, Geoff squeezed him. "Let an old man catch his breath, darling." He stroked his hand down Mica's head, tugging gently at one braid.

The touch was almost as good as the fucking. The words that had been swirling around in his head popped out before he could stop them. "Love you I do."

There was no answer, and for a moment, Mica feared he'd ruined everything. Then he heard a soft snore and understood his husband had fallen asleep.

Mica wasn't sure if he were happy or sad about that. *Both, really.* While he wanted to express his feelings, he also felt vulnerable saying it too soon. Their life together was just starting. They needed time to get to know each other — and in circumstances that weren't colored by life and death perils. Hopefully the journey they were about to set out on would hold more fun than fear. As there was nothing to do about any of it, he relaxed against Geoff's broad chest and let himself drift off.

* * * *

Mica stuffed some of the bread and cheese Alyn had left for them that morning into his mouth as he watched his husband washing himself with avid interest. The water had grown cold because Geoff had insisted Mica use what his sister had also left for them first. The lack of warmth didn't seem to bother the large man. He just got on with the task of removing the remnants of their lovemaking with energetic efficiency and vigor. Mica envied the man. His own energy had flagged with the simple effort of dressing himself, and he wanted to lie down and take a nap as if he were Lye's age and not a fully grown man. Not that he worried about it... The reason for his tiredness made him happy. His first night with his new husband had been one spent more awake than asleep.

And it wasn't only Geoff who was to blame. Mica had turned to him as much as being drawn into his husband's embrace. The first time, he'd been unsure of his welcome. He had no idea what men typically expected of their wives or if they liked them being bold. Sure, Geoff had let him take the lead that once in the cave. They'd been only lovers, though, and the circumstances dire. There might be different rules when married. He'd taken the risk and clasped Geoff's arms before rolling them both over. Of course, he'd only managed to move the heavier body because Geoff had helped him with it. And he didn't have to explain when he spread his legs to permit his husband to lie between them. He'd wanted to look at his husband's face while they fucked. He hadn't even been sure it would work, yet it had. The discomfort of being breached quickly and with no additional cream had been nothing compared to the exquisite pleasure of opening himself up and letting the man in. The ride had been slow and careful, building the climax with unhurried thrusts. And Geoff had kissed him all the while, his tongue in sync with his cock. The mere memory of it made him hard again.

Geoff eyed him as his head popped out of the top of the long shirt Alyn had likely borrowed from her potter friend. Men of the People usually kept their chests mostly bare except when exposed to flying bits such as sparks, wood and clay. Geoff's fair skin, however, needed protection from the sun, and with all his clothes being used up in the cave, he was forced to dress as one of them. Mica thought it a shame to cover up so much enticing muscle, but he didn't want his husband to suffer to satisfy his lust. He supposed the man had thought the same thing when Mica had trapped his dick in a thong and wrapped his new manly kilt around his hips. Geoff wasn't shy about admitting how much he liked looking at him.

"If you keep staring at me, wife, I'm going to have to undress and mount you, and we'll have to start the process of making ourselves presentable all over again."

Mica couldn't help fluttering his lashes. "So bad would that be?"

Geoff chuckled. "Oh darling, you do tempt a man. You must be sore, though, so I'll control myself and leave you alone."

Mica wiggled his butt. There was some discomfort, his ass not being used to being plowed. Still, he couldn't say he minded, given what the reward was for ignoring it. "Other things there are that we might do," he was bold enough to say. "A lot from you I've learned, husband." He licked his lips with deliberate provocation and practiced the pattern of speech he wanted to adopt. "I can feast on something better than this food."

Geoff rewarded him with a grunt, as if he'd been punched in the stomach. "What have I done? You are turning into an insatiable creature." His quick grin told Mica the man was teasing. "And hearing you speak as a Moorcondian is surprisingly arousing."

Mica fluttered his eyelashes some more. "I am the perfect wife for you, I think." He frowned at his lap and concentrated harder. "But if you are determined to leave me, eat something first." He held out a piece of fruit. "Date?"

Geoff approached him slowly, like an animal on the hunt. Squatting before him, he opened his mouth and waited for Mica to put the treat in it. Then he grabbed Mica's hand before he could take it back, chewed, swallowed and sucked the fingers and thumb that had touched the date. All the while, he gazed into Mica's eyes with a heat that, along with the touch, caused him to shiver.

Geoff let him go, picked up a piece of bread-wrapped cheese and rose. "You should get some sleep, darling. You look tired, and as we'll be leaving soon, I trust your village understands not to expect you to do any more labor on their behalf."

Mica felt a pang of sadness. "Duties I have still. Master Noshi I must see. Leave today must we?" he asked, trying not to show how difficult it was going to be for him to leave his home.

Geoff's expression turned serious. "No. Tomorrow is soon enough, but I can't wait any longer than that. I have to assume my men have continued on our journey as instructed. We need to catch up to them." He paused and looked away for a moment. "You don't have to come. If staying with the People is important to you, I can leave you here and hope to see you on the return journey."

Mica jumped to his feet and threw himself against his husband. "No! With you I go." He pulled back to look the man in the eye. "I want to go see the world out there." He hoped he'd gotten the words right because he wanted no misunderstanding on this point. It wasn't merely his lifelong desire to explore what was beyond the People's land. Separating from Geoff now that he knew what it was like to be with a man and mindful of the love he kept hiding in his heart would be intolerable. As much as he loved his family, there really was no choice.

Geoff cupped the back of his neck. "If you're sure?" When Mica nodded, the man kissed him once and stepped away. "I'll speak with your chief and return as quickly as I can. I'll trust you'll do the same. Maybe we can take a little nap together, hmm?"

Mica could only nod enthusiastically, emotions making it hard to speak. When Geoff was gone, he went about straightening the small dwelling and covering the remainder of the food to keep the bugs away. But he didn't have to clear everything out just yet. They could stay here for one more night. It would be their last chance at having real privacy for a long, long time, he assumed. He would make quick work of discussing with Master Noshi what needed to be done once he was gone. Time alone with his husband was going to be a precious thing.

He wondered what it was going to be like, living and traveling with Geoff's men. Mica had never spent much time surrounded by warriors. He expected the Moorcondians took their pleasure with each other and cared not who heard or saw what. Did that mean Geoff would do the same with him, expose him to the others while they pleasured each other? No, he didn't think so. Geoff treated him with the utmost care. Likely he'd make the time and effort for them to steal some privacy somewhere, somehow.

"Being a good little wife, you are?"

Mica whirled around at the sound of the question, his heart thumping painfully. "Lonan, for what reason come you here? Welcome you are not." He took a step back, not liking the warrior's expression. It was his usual cruel one with something more…hunger.

Lonan came farther into the dwelling. "Surprised I am that the cave-in you survived. Now take you I will instead of killing you. A sign the Earth Mother has given me."

Mica's mind whirled with the effort to understand what the man meant. "No sense do your words make."

"Think you that with the man I would let you go? Mine you are...always. Back to me the mountain has given you."

Mica shook his head and took another step back, aware that he had nowhere to go. "Yours I am not. To Sir Geoffrey Arbuthnott I belong." He lifted his chin. "I am his wife."

The slap came so quickly and unexpectedly, Mica couldn't avoid it. His eyes watered from the pain of the blow, but he wouldn't give Lonan the satisfaction of raising his hand to his cheek. Instead, he glared back at him with fisted hands by his side, trying to keep from panting out his fear.

"The People's tongue you will speak. When away from here we are, a lesson I will teach you." The man raised his hand again, in case the meaning wasn't clear.

Realizing how dangerous his situation really was, Mica did the only thing left for him. He opened his mouth to scream for help. This time when Lonan struck, it was to clamp a hand over Mica's mouth and crush his back to the man's chest. Mica struggled to get free, yet he was no match for the warrior's strength.

Lonan pressed his lips close to Mica's ear. "Into the cave the rocks I sent. Died, you and the enemy should have. Surprised I was to see you, and angry I was to see you wedded to him. Your first I should have been. Tainted he has made you. Cleanse you of him I will...soon. Leave we will now. Having you I want more than staying with the People. Together the outside we shall explore, as wanted you always have."

Mica shook his head as much as the hold would allow. *Not with you!*

Lonan tightened his grip and bucked against Mica, letting him feel his erection. "Happy to take my cock you will be. More powerful than he I am."

Mica worked to keep his mounting terror in check. Panicking wasn't going to help him. He processed quickly that Lonan was confessing to somehow causing the cave-in. The idea was inconceivable but a distraction at the moment. What mattered more was that Lonan had decided that Mica's surviving the mountain was somehow a sign that he should take Mica and leave the village, dragging Mica with him. As much as Mica longed for adventure, he would never agree to doing so with Lonan. That was true, even if he weren't already married to Geoff. His mind raced with trying to figure out what to do next.

Lonan forced Mica to stop thinking and start struggling again when the man started humping against his ass. "Have you now, I will."

Mica shook his head and tried to kick back and step on the man's feet. Having put on his soft ceremonial boots, he had no noticeable impact. If anything, his efforts seemed to arouse Lonan more. The warrior laughed and tightened his grip to the point that Mica had trouble breathing. Then he propelled Mica face-first against the wall and pinned him there. As much as he hated it, Mica gave up struggling and lay limp within the man's hold, trying to take breath through Lonan's fingers and cringing as that hateful dick rubbed against his ass. Lonan's hot breath bathed his ear, making him shiver in disgust. When the man groaned long and low, he simple held Mica flush against him until his breathing evened out. Mica's stomach lurched with disgust. He had to swallow hard against the bile threatening to erupt. He wanted to cry, had to blink back tears even, but stiffened his spine and soothed himself with the sure knowledge that Geoff would save him. It was nearly laughable that Lonan believed he could best the man.

"Now we go. No trouble shall you cause."

Mica let himself be pulled away from the wall, waiting for his chance to cause a whole lot of trouble. But when he made his move to wrestle free from Lonan's grip, the man whirled him around and lashed out. Mica had no time to scream before there was an explosion of pain, then nothingness.

Chapter Nine

Geoff raised his cup to both the chief and Mica's father, Keme, as he'd finally introduced himself as. "Thank you both. These provisions you are providing are most generous. It will help me and my men make a longer journey with more certainty. On my return to my homeland, I will make sure my king delivers goods you'll find useful in return."

The two men joined him in drinking. He thought he detected a thawing of their demeanor — not exactly warm but accepting at least. Mica's male relatives hadn't been shy about showing their distrust of him. He couldn't blame them. He was, after all, a trespasser who lived simply because their son and nephew had been willing to vouch for him. That was not the best of circumstances to use as the foundation of any family connection. He'd gained some points by seeing Mica safely out of the cave, naturally — or so he assumed.

The real progress, however, was in how readily he agreed to their demands with respect to Mica's future.

The men had seemed almost indifferent to what Moorcondia might give them, but they were looking out for the boy's interests — and he was glad they were. It was easy to reassure them that he could and would provide for his wife and protect him, as well as promise that there would be a visit on the return trip. All of that had been a given as far as he was concerned. It mattered to them, however, that they had raised these issues as a point of bargaining, and Geoff had agreed as if he were giving something up rather than satisfying his own expectations. Understanding pride and duty, he didn't mind letting these men think they'd won something.

They finished their meal in companionable silence for the most part as the life of the village bustled around them. Everything was happening out in the open, the chief having a spot near the base of the cliffs that offered shade, not far from the dais. A tightly woven blanket gave some relief from the hard ground, and a woman had laden it with all manner of food and jugs of fresh water. Everyone who passed them shot a sideway gaze without raising the ire of the chief, curiosity being acceptable, apparently. No one tried to actively join the discussion or stop to listen, but he would bet that the terms of the negotiation were already being spread around. He appreciated the openness of it, truth be told. The People had their hierarchy and customs like everyone else, yet seemed to be a more egalitarian society than Moorcondia or any other country he'd visited. Geoff made a mental note to keep Mica apprised of all his decisions, because he wanted the boy's adjustment to his new life to be as easy as possible. Plus, he wasn't one of Geoff's men. He even wasn't like Professor Johns. Mica was his wife, and wives deserved consideration that applied to no others.

Keme polished off his drink and rose. "To the stables we go. The pack horses Master Noshi must choose."

Geoff joined him with a nod, hiding his disappointment. "Certainly." Of course it was necessary to get everything sorted out this day to be ready for the next. He couldn't shake the feeling he should be with Mica, however. Telling himself it was just his dick being keen to rejoin its happiest place inside his wife, he schooled himself into patience. Then it occurred to him that Mica might still be at the stables, and he followed his father-in-law with more enthusiasm.

He'd had a chance to visit his horse prior to the marriage ceremony, so he knew the stable master was a man to trust with his mount. Still, it was good to see the beast happily munching on grain when he arrived. A horse that he recognized as being Mica's was in the same corral, and once again, Geoff approved of Noshi's handling of his duties. He was making sure the two mounts were familiar with each other. They would be spending a lot of time together, after all.

Keme met the approaching stable master and wasted no time explaining what provisions were being offered that would require two additional horses to carry. Geoff had done a mental calculation and had determined that the wagon and pack horses that they already had wouldn't be able to hold the extra burden. He was surprised and grateful that he could get two horses, although as he got a good look around for the first time, he noted that the People had quite a lot of them. The most prominent members of their village, such as Mica's family, probably had a mount each. And the fact that he had been given so much confirmed that Mica was an important member of their community. He hoped the boy saw it that way now. His status had nothing to do with being Geoff's wife. Not here, anyway.

He looked around. "Is Mica here?"

Noshi looked at him with surprise. "Seen your wife I have not. In the marriage dwelling he is still I assumed." There was a twinkle in the man's eyes.

Geoff frowned, unease pricking at the back of his neck. "He said he needed to talk to you to make his leaving easier, I suppose. We'd spoken of meeting there later, but I thought he might still be here. He should have come." *Perhaps he fell back to sleep after all.* Gods, he hoped so.

Not waiting for the other men to respond, Geoff raced away, not bothering to hide his worry as he weaved among people going about their business. As he took the steps up to the dwelling two at a time, he saw Keme keeping up with him. That Mica's father worried as well was not comforting, although he appreciated the support. If it turned out the boy was naked and waiting for him on the pallet... Well, the embarrassment would be a small price to pay for finding his wife safe. Geoff's stomach clenched when he arrived at the mouth of the dwelling to find it empty.

Before he could step inside, Keme stopped him by grabbing his arm. "Wait." The man crouched down and studied the hard-packed dirt floor. "Footsteps here."

Geoff joined him and squinted hard at whatever Mica's father was looking at. He was a fair hand at tracking men's movements through the forest, but he saw little here other than smudges. He asked the obvious question. "Mica's?"

Keme shook his head and pointed at another spot. "No. There my son's are. Different ones here." The man showed his teeth. "Lonan."

Now Geoff's stomach dropped out. "Lonan? Are you sure?" How could the man discern another's footsteps so readily?

Keme nodded and let out a growl. "Yes." He put one finger on the ground. "This worn boot mark Lonan's is." He looked at Geoff. "Struggle there was."

Impressed at the man's ability and terrified at the implication of what he said, Geoff had to force himself to calm down. Mica needed him, and losing control wasn't going to help. He didn't need, either, to be told Mica hadn't gone willingly. Although he hadn't been entirely sure he'd heard Mica say the words Geoff remembered as he'd drifted off to sleep, now he was. *Mica loves me.* That wasn't his mind playing tricks. His wife had said it, and Geoff regretted not raising the issue that morning when he'd had the chance. He'd thought he'd wait until they were satiated from lovemaking that night to talk about it. He was going to declare his own love, too. The thought that he might never get the chance to do so horrified him.

Stepping back, he scanned the area outside. "Which way did they go?" He thought he knew but wanted to defer to the expert.

Keme confirmed by gesturing to the right, the side that went away from the village. As there was only one path to take, they hurried along and up the last set of stairs onto the plateau above. Geoff knew where to head without Keme telling him. By a scraggly tree, hoof prints dotted the ground.

Keme studied them. "Two horses. Lonan's and another."

"But not Mica's, because it was at the stables."

Keme's next words didn't help Geoff's worry. "On one horse sits two. Packs the other horse carries."

Geoff had to grit his teeth to keep from howling at the image of Mica trapped in the fucker's arms. "We need to follow. What's the fastest way back to the stables?"

Mica's father said nothing. He merely led Geoff with a grim face back to where Geoff's and Mica's horse were being kept. Master Noshi surprised them by having Geoff's horse and one other already tied to posts and waiting for them. Geoff's tack was lying against the fence beside him.

"Need these you will," Noshi said even before they reached him. "Gone is Lonan's horse."

"Thank you." Hating to take the time to tack up, Geoff did so anyway. He didn't have the skill of the People to easily ride without it and his horse wasn't used to responding to bareback anyway.

The stable master surprised him again by handing over a large knife. "Require this you will."

Geoff hadn't even noticed that his weapons hadn't been returned to him because he'd felt safe here once the beheading problem had been resolved. He took the offering without hesitation and shoved it into the simple braided belt he'd been given along with the clothing and boots. The People really had accepted him as one of their own. He would have to make a point to acknowledge his gratitude over that—once Mica was safe.

Mounting up, Geoff nodded to Keme to take the lead, because the man knew where he was going. It was critical that they wasted no more time. Once they caught up with their quarry, however, he assumed it was a given that Lonan was *his* to deal with. It didn't matter what kind of punishment the People might reserve for this kind of criminal act. The man would pay for this transgression with his life.

* * * *

Mica's head ached so badly he thought it might roll off his shoulders. There was a throbbing along his right cheek, and that side of his jaw that was unlike any pain he'd ever known. No one had hit him before, not in the face, let alone so hard that he'd passed out. It took effort for him to open his eyes, and as he did, he took stock of his situation. Memories of what had happened and understanding of his current predicament flooded in. He stiffened and struggled instinctively once he realized he was mounted on a horse in front of Lonan. The warrior's grip around his waist was too tight for him to move much at all.

"Still you will be," the man barked. "Or tie you across the pack horse I will."

Knowing his stomach and head would suffer greatly from being upside down, he worked to get himself under control. He cringed at the feel of Lonan's hard dick pressing against his back. As bad it was and as bad as what had happened in the cave had been, he knew that far worse was in store for him once Lonan decided to stop and rest—except that wasn't going to happen. Geoff was coming after him. He was certain of that and was surprised that Lonan didn't seem worried about it. Was he truly so convinced that the Earth Mother blessed his actions that he held no concern about being followed and stopped?

Their pace was slow and steady, not a rush to escape. His head hurt worse with the effort to reason out Lonan's thinking—that was assuming there was any rational thought going on at all. A stab of pain at his temple made him wince. It was then that he noticed where they were. He'd never seen the place before. It was a narrow canyon hemmed in on either side by high rock walls. It was barely wide enough for both animals to walk through side-by-side, tethered as the pack horse was to Lonan's mount.

"Where are we?" He barked out a cry when Lonan dug his fingers into his side.

"Speak not like him!"

Mica hadn't even realized he'd been using Geoff's mode of speech. It pleased him how easily it had come out, but he dared not aggravate his captor. He needed to bide his time. "This place is where? Know it I do not."

Lonan loosened his grip. "A route through the mountain I found one day long ago. Told no one I did. Secret it is."

Mica expected that was true. He'd never heard of a way through the mountain as a means of escaping the village during a raid. And the chief wouldn't have kept such an important piece of information to himself. If it was a way out, it was a way in, and warriors didn't guard the plateau. So yes, it was entirely likely that Lonan was the only one who had stumbled upon this route, although it hardly mattered. They'd be followed if they weren't being already. Even if Geoff had trouble tracking them, his father would not. If Lonan believed that his family would be happier with his being carted off by a warrior than married to an outsider, he was sick in the mind. And his pride of purpose and belief in his own cleverness went beyond what a normal warrior would possess.

As the pain in his head and face abated, we wondered if he dared use Lonan's cockiness against him to slow their progress. It was worth a try. The worst that would happen would be another painful chastisement. He knew he could take it.

"Thirsty I am. Water might I have?" There were skins attached only to the pack animal, so they would have to stop for some amount of time for Lonan to grab one.

His captor didn't answer right away. Then, "Ask me nicely you will."

Knowing that what the man really meant was for him to beg for it, Mica complied. His pride didn't matter to him as much as survival and being with his husband again. "Please."

"Nicer," Lonan bit out.

"*Please.*" Mica let some of his fear thread his tone.

That worked. Lonan pulled his horse to a stop and let go of Mica in order to reach for a water skin. Mica was careful not to make any move that implied he was using the request as a ruse, because he wasn't doing that. He'd never outrun Lonan on foot, let alone while he was on horseback. All he wanted was to give Geoff more time to catch up with them. And he really was thirsty. His mouth tasted like blood from where he must have bitten his tongue when Lonan had punched him. His throat was raw as well. The day was hot, and this route through the mountain afforded no shade and allowed little wind to reach them so far.

He tried to take the skin from Lonan once he had it in hand, but the man held on to it tightly and forced him to accept the drink under his control. He was prepared for the asshole to try to tease it away or tip the skin too much to flood his mouth. Lonan did neither, either pleased by Mica's meekness or smart enough still to conserve their provisions. It was possible the man had no idea how far the canyon went or where it led. The thought of it was frightening. They might run out of water and food before Lonan realized they had to turn back, not that he ever would do so. If what he'd said about causing the cave-in was right, he was prepared to kill out of spite and maybe even prepared to die, as well.

After taking a swig himself, Lonan returned the skin to its tie and sent the horse walking once more. "A good boy you shall be and more will be given."

"Understand I do." He kept his head down and his voice soft. Inside, though, he was screaming for Geoff to hurry.

* * * *

"Wait!" Geoff brought his horse to a stop and stared at the pile of rock to the left of the fissure in the mountain they were about to enter. It was far to the right of the cave entrance, not visible unless one went exploring. From Keme's expression, he gathered no one had. A religious restriction perhaps. Even as every fiber of his body egged him to keep going, he knew it was important to understand what he was seeing.

He jumped off and handed Keme his reins, then climbed as much as he could to get a look at what he judged to be part of the mountain that lay at the mouth of the cave. There were boulders piled precariously to one side. He'd seen this natural configuration before. Water carved rock randomly, creating piles here and there—some stable, some not. A huge boulder sat embedded deeply into the ground. A scatter of smaller rocks around the hole indicated they'd been kicked up when it had fallen.

"What see you?" Keme called out.

"I'm not sure." Except he was. Eyeing a stout branch nearby, he lifted it to judge its strength and study the markings on its bark. Could this have been used? He scoured the remaining boulders above him and pictured wedging the branch under the topmost one. *Yes, this would do it.*

Dropping the piece of wood, he remounted his horse. "Do you know this place?"

Keme shook his head. "Here we do not go. A surprise to me it is."

Geoff rather thought it was. The People had their customs, and the mouth of the mountain had a role in that. But their lives were lived on the plateau, the cliffs and the ground beneath it all. They wouldn't have any reason to explore the parts at a higher elevation, so wouldn't have known how precarious the cave's existence really was. Lonan had, though. For whatever reason, the fucker had scoped out this area and had seen the possibilities. But for Mica's choice to marry Geoff and make him his guide, the man might never have had a need or desire to exploit the knowledge. As insane as it seemed, he guessed the man would rather Mica have died than belong to someone else. This knowledge was merely one more reason to kill him. It also gave him a new sense of urgency. If Lonan had been willing to kill once… He wouldn't hesitate to do so again if he became cornered and thought it was his only option.

"We must pick up speed." Kicking his horse, he headed into the narrow canyon as fast as he dared.

It wasn't easy to navigate because the ground was littered with rocks that must constantly fall from the walls with no travelers to clear them. His horse was smart enough to pick its way carefully, and he was forced to stop trying to make it ignore its own sense of survival in favor of his commands. They'd gone far into the space, so much so that Geoff couldn't see the mouth of it when he looked over his shoulder. He worried though that instead of overtaking their quarry, they were losing time that had been gained by their swift arrival to the entrance of the canyon. Lonan might be going at an equally slow pace, but his head start gave him an advantage. *How far have they gotten?*

"Geoffrey."

He stopped abruptly, more out of surprise at hearing his name spoken by Keme for the first time than any sense that is what the man expected. He turned to watch Mica's father ride up to his side. "What is it? Do you see or hear something?"

"No. Change horses we must."

Geoff blinked at him and furrowed his brow. "Why?"

"More sure-footed my horse is. Faster you will go."

He frowned. The desert-dweller was right. The People left their mounts unshod so the beasts were used to traversing this mountainous terrain without the slippery effect of the horseshoe. Certainly, Keme's horse appeared more at ease than his own, standing still while his mount stomped and skittered around.

Switching horses made sense if Geoff was to be the one to challenge Lonan, except there was one problem.

"I can't ride bareback with no tack." He held up his reins to make his point clear.

Keme merely shrugged and dismounted. "The mane you hold and figure it out you will. Always a warrior does when necessary."

Damn, the man was right. In the face of Mica's danger, he could manage anything to save him. And the fact that Keme had just complimented him by acknowledging his warrior status was not lost on him. Geoff wasted no more time, getting off his mount and throwing himself onto the back of the desert horse. He'd ridden without a saddle before. All soldiers had to learn to. It was the steering that worried him. Then again, there was nowhere to go other than straight through the path worn into the rock.

He grabbed a fistful of mane with one hand in the same manner he'd seen the others do. "I will find him."

With that firm promise, he kicked his mount forward.

* * * *

It was hard for Mica to keep his energy and his spirits up. There was still no doubt in his mind that Geoff was coming for him. But after hours of travel, he feared his husband would not reach him in time to stop Lonan from doing what he clearly wanted to. It took no imagination to anticipate what that was, either. The fucker kept up a steady stream of explicit descriptions of what he was going to do to Mica and what he expected Mica to do in return. In his way of saying it, everything sounded disgusting, nothing like the loving sharing of pleasure he'd known with Geoff. If Lonan had his way, Mica would be a slave to the man's whims and lead a life of torture in the man's quest to slake his thirst for Mica's body.

It won't come to that.

The worst that he would endure would be one night before Geoff caught up with them and killed Lonan. Mica was sure of the outcome, and with each step of the horse, his own desire to see the man's blood spilled grew. He was not a violent person, but Lonan had violated him already, enough so that he could feel no pity for the man. His hope was that Geoff's touch would wash away the stench of Lonan's lust. Except...what if Geoff didn't want him anymore now that Lonan had used him for his pleasure, even in a way that hadn't violated his body with possibly worse to come? He shook his head at the notion. Geoff was a man of honor. He wouldn't cast him aside or blame him for what had happened.

"What?" Lonan demanded.

It took Mica a moment to realize his head movement had caught the man's attention. That had been stupid of him. Despite needing to pee and the ache in his ass and thighs from riding so long after a night of losing his virginity, he'd dared not ask for them to stop. Once they dismounted, he judged Lonan wouldn't be able to control himself. He'd want to take advantage of the time, however short, to give in to his needs.

"A fly is all."

Lonan slid his hand down from Mica's waist to cup his groin. "No, I think. A rest you want." He squeezed Mica's cock in emphasis.

Desperate to dissuade him, Mica said, "Fine I am."

"What you are I say. Stop we will."

There was no help for it now. Lonan had made up his mind. He tugged his horse to a stop, forcing the pack one to, as well, dismounted and helped Mica down, whether he wanted it or not. Truth be told, he was unsteady and needed support to keep his knees from buckling. That didn't stop him from cringing as Lonan held him upright until his legs were firmer.

His captor cupped Mica's chin. "Relieve yourself, then my turn it is." The nasty grin on his face conveyed what kind of 'turn' he was intending.

Wrenching free, Mica stumbled over to the nearest wall and leaned against it. He was loath to expose himself to Lonan's predatory gaze. But as the man was tending to the horses, giving them water and not staring at Mica. Plus, he judged any resistance to be futile. He turned to face the wall and freeing his dick, he closed his eyes to relax sufficiently to let his urine flow.

It did feel good to empty his bladder, but he quickly shoved his thong in place when he heard Lonan's soft footfalls approaching. As much as he wanted to cower against the rock, he turned to face the man.

He saw his immediate future in the gleam of the man's eyes and the bulge that showed within his kilt. Mica raised his chin and tried not to flinch when Lonan shoved his kilt to one side and reached to untie his thong.

Mica's nerves wore out at that moment, and he threw caution to the wind. "Hate you I do."

Lonan bared his teeth. "Fight me then. Better your struggles will make it."

Mica's stomach dropped. There was nothing he could do. Lonan was determined to hurt him, and humiliation was part of his plan, not merely satisfying his long-held lust. He fought back tears and whimpers, determined at least to not give the fucker any more satisfaction than he had to.

The warrior stopped before he freed himself, however. He froze, then let go of his ties to turn in the direction they had come. Mica did as well, realizing that the warrior's well-honed hearing had detected the sound of a horse's hooves before Mica had. Now he heard the brisk *clop, clop* and a figure appeared around a bend. Mica's heart leaped at the sight. He would have recognized it as being Geoff, even if he hadn't been sure that his husband was coming for him. The man from the faraway land sat taller than any warrior of the People ever could—his size imposing, his power obvious. Geoff had seen them, too, because he prodded his mount to a faster trot.

For a few seconds as Geoff approached, Lonan made no move. Then whipping out his knife, he made a grab for Mica. He'd had the instinct to dance away at the moment he'd seen the warrior go for his weapon. His quick reaction meant Lonan closed his fingers around nothing but air. The man snarled and lunged for him. Once more, Mica dodged his attack. The uneven ground proved his downfall, however. He tripped off balance as he stepped on a rock, and that gave Lonan an opening. He dug his fingers into Mica's arm hard enough to make him cry out, and he whirled him around to press his back against Lonan's chest. The knife blade stopped a hair's breadth from Mica's throat. He dared not struggle in the face of that jeopardy.

"Halt! Or kill him I will." Lonan's tone left no doubt he meant what he said.

Geoff pulled his horse to a stop and slid off its back as if he'd been born to ride as a warrior of the People.

He took a few steps toward them, then froze when Lonan hiked Mica closer to him.

Geoff held out his hands. "I won't come closer. I know you'll follow through on your threat. The man who tried to bury the boy alive is too selfish to do otherwise when he knows he can't keep him."

Mica wasn't surprised at the accusation of causing the cave-in, because Lonan had bragged as much already. He wondered how his husband knew, however.

Lonan was curious, too. "How know you this?"

"It wasn't hard to see once you led us to this untrod path. It must have been hard to dislodge that rock, and you couldn't have known for sure it would cause a cave-in."

"Strong I am and mattered not if unsuccessful it was." He jerked Mica in his hold. "Always had I another plan. Showed me the way, the Earth Mother did."

Geoff lowered his hands, although he kept them away from his sides. "Yes, you're clever, I'll grant you that. No one else ever bothered to explore the mountain, but you did, although I find it hard to believe your Earth Mother put all of these ideas and options into your head."

"What you think matters not."

"About the deity? Perhaps, but what I think about your villainy matters very much indeed. You're just not accepting it—yet." He jutted his chin toward the way ahead of them. "Do you even know where this leads?"

Lonan shrugged, the gesture causing the knife edge to get even closer to Mica's skin. "Find out we will."

Geoff didn't say anything more for a few seconds. "You know that's not true, not while I still live. There are only two outcomes here. You kill the boy, then yourself, if I don't get to you first...or you kill me here and now. I'm assuming you're not going to simply give me my wife back and flee. And I won't let you leave with him. Surely you understand that."

"A fight you want?"

Geoff lifted his chin. "Of course. We are both warriors, are we not? The winner gets Mica. The loser dies. Men have been doing personal combat since the dawn of time. I'm sure you will make a worthy opponent, and so will I." He bared his teeth.

It seemed as if the air grew tense with the following silence. Lonan was restless, an outward sign that he wasn't as confident in himself as he would have everyone believe. His grip around Mica tightened before he suddenly flung him aside. Mica had to put up his hands to stop from crashing into the canyon wall. He whirled to lean against it, his heart pounding and panting with fear. It didn't matter if he was out of immediate danger. Geoff was heading into it. He couldn't bear watching him fight Lonan and yet couldn't tear his gaze away from it.

The two men met in the space in between them, away from the horses, giving them as much room as the narrow path allowed. Lonan was skilled with a knife, this Mica knew. He had to assume Geoff was as well, except he'd only ever seen the man with a short one stuck in his belt. What he'd called a sword was longer than any knife, but that weapon had been left behind with his men. The advantage it would have given him wasn't available. This kind of warfare required close quarters. And with that thought, Mica suddenly understood that the advantage still belonged to Geoff. As long as his arms were, he had greater reach than

Lonan. Unless the fucker fought dirty—which was a certainty—odds favored Geoff as the victor. Mica tried to catch his husband's attention before he engaged with Lonan to show his confidence in him. But Geoff's gaze never wavered from his opponent.

They circled each other around and around before Lonan struck.

Chapter Ten

Geoff strained to resist the temptation to look at his wife. It was a distraction he couldn't afford. He'd seen enough to know that the boy was able to stand on his own power, so he had to hope he wasn't too badly hurt. The livid bruise on his wife's face made his blood boil, but that would heal. It was the possible damage under his kilt that worried him. All hurts would fade over time — even emotional ones — if he was a good husband to Mica, however. He had to believe that. And gutting his captor might go a long way to helping as well. Mica was such a sweet boy by nature that he probably didn't hunger for revenge the way Geoff did. Then again, he'd glimpsed the emotion behind his wife's eyes. There was fear, naturally, but also hatred. Lonan's end might not bother him overly much, if at all.

He'd left it to Lonan to take the first swipe, and the fucker had not disappointed, his impatience overriding his judgment — to the extent he had any — very quickly. Being more patient than one's opponent was always the right strategy in personal combat. He was comfortable, too, fighting with a knife instead of a sword. His training as a Moorcondian soldier had been comprehensive. Being older than the desert warrior gave him a leg up in that control, as well. Plus, he wasn't rabid-ass crazy, and given the look in Lonan's eyes, he was sure the man was. His judgment from the start had been bizarre, and Geoff could only hope that failing continued with his fighting strategy.

He dodged Lonan's next swipe, then pivoted to lash out himself. Having the longer arms meant that Geoff didn't have to get as close to the other man to strike him. A hiss and a bloom of blood told him he'd hit his mark, although it wasn't the knife arm. The gash on Lonan's biceps looked deep, yet it wouldn't bleed sufficiently to slow the asshole down. So, Geoff made them circle some more to deplete Lonan's energy.

The man sneered. "Afraid you are."

Geoff nearly grinned at the effort. He hadn't let a taunt goad him into acting since his very first lesson had been when the instructor insulted every bit of his manhood and ended with a nasty crack about Geoff's mother. When he'd lashed out in anger, the man had knocked him easily on his ass. *Lesson learned.* Perhaps Lonan hadn't had a comparable experience with whoever had trained him—or he had and it hadn't stuck, because he was arrogant in addition to being insane.

He put the theory to the test. "Of whom should I be afraid, a man too low among the People to seduce Mica properly? Why would he—the son of the shaman and the nephew of the chief—want a nothing like you? Even a stranger held more appeal for him."

It was the right sore spot to hit, and as predicted, the asshole took the bait. With his face scrunched in fury,

Lonan lunged at him. His blade got close enough to cut Geoff's shirt but missed even grazing his skin. His thrust was truer, slashing Lonan's side. The man stumbled back out of reach, closing his hand over the wound. The arm of his knife hand wavered before he managed to raise it again.

Lonan's bravado came back. "Worse I've had."

Doubtful. Geoff allowed the bastard to think he was fooled by stepping farther away from him and circling once more, but the fight was almost over. He had the upper hand now and needed only a little more patience. A man about to lose was like a cornered animal — at their most dangerous. Geoff couldn't afford to let his guard down so close to victory. So he waited again until Lonan couldn't resist another strike. When he did, Geoff weaved to one side and dropped his own weapon to take him down hand-to-hand. The desert warrior wasn't expecting that and was therefore unable to counter Geoff's move. He snapped the wrist of the knife hand, sending the blade clattering to the ground. He tumbled Lonan onto his back and followed him to pin his arms.

The man proved slipperier than he'd expected and managed to evade his grabbing of the blood-soaked hand. Lonan snarled at him. "Over this is not."

If the hand hadn't been so visible because of the blood, Geoff might have missed where it was going. He rolled off Lonan and jumped away from him just as the man pulled a small knife from his boot. It had been well-hidden and not of much more use than carving meat off a carcass, but it would have very ably punctured Geoff's jugular vein. He crouched out of reach, breathing harshly and ready for the weapon to be thrown at him.

In the end, Lonan proved himself to be more or less of a warrior than expected, depending on how one viewed it. Straining his neck in order to gaze at Mica, who remained plastered against the wall, Lonan jammed the knife into his neck. It wasn't the fastest way to go but with such a small blade, it was the surest place to strike and be certain it would do the job. As blood spurted out of him, the man kept his eyes open as long as he could, staring at Mica. Soon after he closed them, he was dead.

Geoff was sure Lonan was no longer a danger, yet he followed his training and made sure to remove all the knives from his reach and to see that none more lurked within his boots. And with the amount of blood spilled and the stillness of the man's body, it was clear he was truly gone. Only then did Geoff give in to what he needed to do. He walked over to Mica and stayed the impulse to grab him into a smothering hug. The boy had to be in shock still, and Geoff didn't want to overwhelm him. Instead, he brushed his thumb against the bruise on the boy's face, tracing it from his cheekbone to his jaw. It was obvious seeing it up close that his wife had been hit at least twice, one of which would have knocked him out.

"I would have killed him for this alone." Dropping his hand, he added, "Come and let me tend to..." He had the breath knocked out of him as his wife flew in to wrap his arms around Geoff's neck. Without hesitation, Geoff enfolded him in an embrace.

"Scared I was for you." Mica's voice was muffled against Geoff's skin.

"Darling, I was never going to let that fucker keep or kill you. The outcome of our fight was pre-ordained."

"Knew you would come I did. Hope I had always."

Geoff smiled into Mica's hair. "Your confidence in me is humbling, but yes, there was never any question that I would track you down once I realized what had happened."

At the sound of hooves approaching, Mica stiffened. Geoff pried them apart so that Mica could see who was coming.

"Don't worry. It's only your father."

"Came with you he did?"

The surprise in Mica's tone made his heart squeeze. "Of course, he did. Without his tracking skills, I would have had a lot harder time locating you."

Keme dismounted and walked over to Lonan's corpse. He peered down at it as if to make doubly sure the man was dead, then spat on it before approaching Geoff and Mica. The look on the man's face softened as he gazed at his son. Like Geoff had, Keme ran his thumb along Mica's bruise and grunted.

"Glad I am he is dead. Proud I am of you for surviving."

A sob tore out of Mica, and he went from Geoff's arms to Keme's. Geoff didn't mind. He had the rest of his life to enjoy his wife's attention and was pleased to see the two men share affection. From what Mica had said, it was obvious they had struggled to bond. It was heartwarming to see the father and son hugging.

Keme broke the hug. "Well you have done. Now take care of that offal I must." He gestured toward Lonan.

"I'll help." First, Geoff took Mica by the shoulders. "You should sit, darling, and rest. Would you like some water." Mica nodded. "Here... This is a good spot."

He placed Mica on a flattish rock close to the wall, turning him so that he couldn't see the body. Then he retrieved the water skin from the pack horse Lonan had provisioned and brought it back to Mica. It pleased him when his wife drank deeply.

He patted Mica's shoulder, feeling inadequate to help his wife now that the fight was over. Caretaking was not something he was used to, not when emotions were at stake. Give him a problem to resolve, like the time in the cave or the chase out here to rescue him, and he was in his element. But with his tears drying, Mica's face had taken on a vacant look that scared him.

"I won't be long."

Geoff helped Keme with the dirty job of slinging Lonan's body across the horse Lonan had ridden. The poor creature was not happy, given the scent of blood on the corpse, but they managed to tie it tight.

Keme grimaced. "To his parents I will take him. Ashamed they will be."

"For what it's worth, I don't think he was right in the head. No one sane would do as he had."

"Right you may be." He clasped Geoff on the shoulder. "Mica you will bring now?"

Geoff glanced at his wife, happy to see he wasn't watching the gruesome clean-up as Geoff had hoped. "No. He's been through a lot these last days and needs rest before riding for so long again." He glanced up at the sky. "Night is falling. Are you sure you want to make the journey in the dark?"

Keme patted his horse's neck. "Steady she is and the way home she knows, no matter from where." He glanced in Mica's direction. "My son you take care of."

"Always."

Once Keme was gone, Geoff stared at the blood-soaked ground and decided that here was not the place to make camp. After he tethered the pack horse to his own, he walked over to his wife and crouched in front of him. "We're going to spend the night in the canyon to give us both some time to rest...but not here. We'll make a short journey homeward first. Do you want to walk or ride?" He figured all the boy's muscles would be sore, and any movement was going to hurt. As much as it pained him, Geoff couldn't carry him and control two horses at the same time.

Mica drank some more water before answering. "Walk I'd rather." He blinked hard a few times. "Tired I am, so not too far, please."

"Not too far, I promise." *Just to a point where this hideous spot can no longer be seen.* "We'll stop where it looks good for making camp."

Taking Mica's hand, he helped him to his feet and over to the horses. He was careful to keep his body between his wife and the spot where Lonan had died as much as possible. He grabbed his horse's reins while keeping hold of his wife's hand. The pace was set by Mica's slow walk, which was as it should be. The boy's gait was steady, although every step appeared labored. Geoff feared that difficulty had more to do with Mica's emotions than his physical fatigue.

Fortunately there were enough larger boulders along the way that it didn't take long to find a spot where there was some protection from the wind that was starting to pick up with night descending. Geoff went about setting up camp, spreading a blanket for Mica to sit on and creating a fire pit. Tumbleweeds were plentiful, and as much of a crazy fucker as Lonan had been, he'd provisioned his packs with everything necessary to live outdoors for a while, including a bit of grain for the horses.

One strike of the flint had fire catching in the weeds. Soon, a bright, warm fire bathed Mica. Having seen to the most important task first, Geoff went to feed and water the horses and hobble them for the night. He unpacked the human food and sat with it beside his wife. Seeing goosebumps on Mica's skin, despite the heat of the blaze, he pulled off his shirt and tugged it over the boy's head. "Here, darling, wear this."

Mica helped by putting his arms through the sleeves. "Cold you will be."

"Not at all. I'm a big man and frankly prefer the coolness of the night to the hotness of the day." He picked up a piece of dried meat. "You must be hungry as much as tired. Try to eat something before you sleep."

Mica took the food without saying anything and bit off a chunk. Then he did something that lightened Geoff's heart. He leaned against Geoff and lay his head on his shoulder as he chewed.

Relieved at the show of trust and affection, Geoff put his arm around his wife and held him close as he ate, as they both did. With the first bite, Geoff realized he was starving. Breakfast had been a long time ago, and of course, he'd had nothing since. He ate with gusto, putting aside any disgust that he was consuming what Lonan had touched. It was critical that he provide an example for his wife, and food was food, after all. It's not like it embodied the evil of the man who had packed it.

When he judged that Mica had eaten enough, he stopped urging him to consume more and simply sat in an easy embrace. The boy yawned and shuddered against him. Geoff kissed the top of the boy's head and maneuvered him to lie down. "It's time for sleep."

But as he tried to let go to tend to the fire, Mica clung to him. "Hold me, please."

Geoff wordless lay beside his wife and held him close. "I won't leave you...ever. I only want to bank the fire...or build it up again if you're still cold."

Mica shook his head and tightened his grip. "Warm you make me."

Geoff entwined his body with his wife's to act as a better blanket. "Is this okay?" He continued to worry that Mica's emotions were running high, and he didn't want to remind him of his time with Lonan. He had no doubt the asshole had forced himself on Mica to some degree. Mica's nod came as a relief. "Please tell me if I upset you in any way, darling. I won't ask you to speak of your ordeal more than you are comfortable with, but I do understand you must be feeling...vulnerable."

Mica said nothing at first, although he ran his fingers across Geoff's chest in a light caress. "Hurt me he did not...much."

Geoff skimmed the boy's bruised cheek. "I disagree, darling."

"Mean I..."

"It's all right. I understand," Geoff was quick to reassure him, while nearly dizzy with relief that his wife hadn't suffered the worst of all possibilities.

Mica's next words, however, broke his heart. "Dirty he made me feel."

Geoff had to take a moment to pull himself together. He was nearly desperate to jump on his horse and catch up to Keme so that he could carve Lonan into little pieces. It was a stupid impulse, but he vibrated with the effort to somehow make the fucker pay all over again for what he'd done to this precious boy.

He found his voice finally and prayed he got the words right. "You are nothing of the sort. You are a brave, resourceful and resilient young man...and my beloved." It was as if a weight had lifted off him in making that confession, except he had to be as explicit as possible so that there would be no misunderstanding. "I love you, Mica."

Mica fluttered his lashes and wetness dropped onto Geoff's skin. "Say that you need not."

Geoff separated their bodies in order for them to look at each other. He framed Mica's face with his hands. "I'm not saying that to make you feel better. I'd intended to make my declaration tonight back when I thought we'd spend it in the wedding dwelling." He licked his lips to give him time to marshal his thoughts. "As I was drifting off to sleep last night, I thought I heard you say that you love me. Was I wrong?"

Mica screwed up his face as more tears leaked from his eyes. "No. I. Love. You, husband. For a while now. Afraid I was to tell you."

"You must never be afraid to tell me anything. Do you understand?" Mica hesitated before nodding. "Good. I will never lie to you, darling, or tell you something simply because I think you want to hear it. When I started on this journey, I wasn't looking for a wife. That's probably obvious," he added with a chuckle he couldn't hold back. "Then there you were. Honestly, I started falling in love with you the moment I saw you in that quicksand. You believe me, don't you?"

Now Mica nodded quickly, and his crying turned into a smile. "Mount me, will you? Now."

Oh, this was a tricky problem. How could he turn down his wife's request without risking undoing all that he'd said?

Geoff pulled them both into a sitting position. Mica looked at him with his arresting beauty that nearly stopped Geoff's heart each time he saw him. "From this point forward, we will speak of what we do in our marriage bed — or on a pallet or blanket or wherever we happen to be — as making love. That is what we are doing, not simply satisfying a carnal need." He closed his eyes briefly. "And we won't be doing that tonight. Only because it would hurt you," he said as Mica's face fell, "and for no other reason."

Geoff lay the boy back down. "You've only lost your virginity last night, and we weren't exactly restrained. Then you spent today on horseback. You are very sore. Don't lie to me," he warned when it looked as if Mica were about to deny it. An idea occurred to him. "Let me wash the grime of the day off you and loosen your muscles before you sleep."

He didn't emphasize that part of what drove him to make the offer was that Mica had used the word 'dirty'. The boy hadn't meant the kind that came from riding all day. They both knew that. But a bath, even a meager one as he could give out here, might help make him feel better. A massage would help ease the soreness that had to be plaguing his legs, at least.

Geoff peered down at Mica, holding his breath, afraid he'd hurt the boy's feelings with his refusal — or worse, made him believe that Geoff didn't really want him anymore. Finally, Mica gave his permission with a quick nod. Geoff smiled before turning to stoke the fire.

There was a sufficient amount of water and the ride back to the village would take less than a day, so he was comfortable sacrificing some of it for bathing. A bowl used to water the horses served as the wash basin, and Geoff cut off a piece of the horse blanket to use as a washcloth. Sadly, there was no soap, but this effort was about making Mica feel clean, regardless of how he smelled. Geoff stoked the fire with more weeds and used it to warm the water. Mica watched him as he did all of it, and the wanted attention gave Geoff a sense of real caretaking for his wife.

When he returned, he started with Mica's upper body. He stripped off the shirt he'd given the boy, wetted the cloth, then began to wash him. He wanted it to be soothing as well as cleansing, so he took his time, sliding the cloth over the boy's face, careful with the bruised side. Next came the neck and shoulders, which Mica held stiffly at first. Under Geoff's tender ministrations, however, the boy visibly relaxed. Geoff kept up a steady stream of information about his family and home, telling tales in a low voice that he hoped was soothing. Mica liked hearing about it all and Geoff figured the normalcy of it would help. Mica lay compliant, letting him raise each arm in turn to wash underneath. Once he was finished, Geoff dressed his wife again with the shirt. The garment was hardly fresh, but it didn't have any blood on it and would keep Mica warm. That was all that was needed.

Geoff moved down to Mica's feet, slipping his boots off. They were so small and slender, almost delicate, except they were calloused, as to be expected as someone who wandered the desert as he did. Once he washed them, Geoff held them on his lap and massaged them, pressing his thumbs into the arches. He didn't have any real skill in it, but he figured he was doing a decent job when his wife moaned in obvious pleasure. It put Geoff in mind of the sounds the boy made when being pleasured in a different way. Geoff had to put those thoughts aside to keep himself from going mad with restraint.

Next, he washed upward to the knee, careful to keep away from the most sensitive spots on the boy's body until the end. He kept his touch brisk and efficient, because Mica seemed to have relaxed quite a bit. Once that was done, he tackled the most enticing bits of his wife's body, the ones that he knew he could make sing with pleasure. Already he was hard himself to nearly bursting. Hands, feet, knees—it didn't matter what he touched. It was all arousing to him. But he was careful to hide it, making sure his erection didn't press against any part of the boy. The last thing he wanted was to appear as if he did this out of his own desire.

He realized his worry was foolish as soon as he untied Mica's kilt. The boy's cock bulged against his thong, clearly interested in playing. Geoff couldn't hold back a grin, and Mica made the same expression, even though his eyes were closed and he couldn't tell what Geoff's reaction had been. Right at that moment, Geoff knew they'd be all right. Mica's ordeal hadn't stifled his interest in sex, and his plea to be mounted hadn't been done to reassure himself that his husband still desired him. Nevertheless, Geoff continued his task with the same slow and measured actions.

Leaving the thong in place, he ran the cloth up and down Mica's thighs. He went so far as to wipe the inner thighs of each leg up to the edge of the leather covering. His wife rewarded him with hitched breath and small shudders. The boy's dick peeked out of the top of its confines, as it typically did, and it was tempting to free it. Geoff made himself wait, to build up Mica's arousal as long as possible. He worked the muscles of each thigh to loosen them from their long time astride a horse. His efforts had the dual effect of relaxing his wife's body while also stimulating him. It was immensely gratifying, and he kept up his ministrations until he judged he had done a good job of both. By the time he untied the string and yanked the thong away, his wife was making mewing sounds, and while his legs were splayed bonelessly, his fingers were curled against the blanket.

"I want to dine on your cock, darling. May I?"

The answer came in the form of a groan and hips bucking up. That was the perfect response. Geoff straddled the boy's lower legs and leaned down on his forearms. The scent of Mica's pre-cum hit his nostrils. He inhaled deeply to savor it before licking a stripe up the shaft from balls to tip. Mica moaned and bucked again, his demand clear. Still, Geoff played with the dick a little more, lapping and teasing the bundle of nerves beneath the cockhead. His own dick throbbed. He ignored it. Now was for Mica only.

When he judged that he'd teased them both sufficiently, he sucked the cock into his mouth. He let it sit on his tongue at first, working the shaft by sucking and laving his tongue around it. He kept a tight grip on the base of his wife's cock to choke off the orgasm. Making it last was something they hadn't yet explored, both of them having been too needy each time they came together to do so. This was different. Time was on their side, and they'd had the chance to experience the best their bodies had to offer. Orgasms that were thwarted for a while were that much more intense. His wife gave him a wordless command by wiggling his hips and trying to buck his cock in farther. Geoff ignored him and continued the teasing.

Finally, as Mica's moans turned into verbal pleas, Geoff let go of the base, inhaled deeply and took the cock all the way into his throat. He only had to swallow once. Mica arched his back as his cum flooded into Geoff. He took it all, drinking every drop, and didn't let go until he'd drained his wife dry.

In the aftermath of Mica's orgasm, Geoff laid the boy's kilt across his lap for warmth and pulled his boots back on. But when he tried to lie down beside him, Mica held him off with a stiff-armed hold on his chest. Alarmed, Geoff searched for what he'd done to make his wife not want him close. Had the blow job been too much after all? The next moment, his worry fled.

Opening his eyes halfway, Mica gave him a fierce look. "Your cock you must feed me, husband. I want to make love to it," he added, changing his syntax in his adorable way.

Geoff cupped his groin where his cock pressed for release. "I fear I am too needy. As much as I want you, I worry I'll be too rough."

"*Never*."

The simple confidence his wife showed in him was humbling. And there was no point in his head overriding what both his cock and his wife demanded. He edged up toward Mica's face, making sure the boy's hands were free and resting on Geoff's thighs. It was important that he not make his wife feel trapped. He tugged off his kilt and thong, appreciating the ease of the native clothing. He might never want to wear trousers again. His dick sprang forth, hard as rock, pulsing with its arousal. It was far too big for his wife's mouth, but he would let the boy set the pace and be careful not to choke him. Clasping the shaft, he tipped it down to Mica's mouth.

His wife opened wide in invitation. Geoff let only the tip in, closing his eyes and groaning at the exquisite velvety warmth that greeted it. He wasn't going to need much effort to come. It wasn't necessary to feed more of the shaft into Mica's mouth. The boy was determined, however, to set the pace and get what he wanted. He lifted his head to press his face forward to capture more of Geoff's dick. Realizing he'd been overruled, Geoff placed his palms on either side of his wife's head and lowered his pelvis. If Mica was going to suck on more of his cock, the least Geoff could do was make it comfortable for him.

Mica accepted the help by laying his head down again. His lips were stretched wide by Geoff's shaft. They looked ready to split in two. The boy's tongue tickled Geoff's slit, causing the dick to pulse more urgently. He wasn't going to last much longer. He thrust shallowly, careful not to go too far. His breath labored with the effort to remain in control, and he bunched the blanket in his fists. Mica threw him suddenly over the edge by scraping his upper teeth along the shaft. With a howl, Geoff threw back his head. He held onto just enough sanity to know he would shove his dick all the way into Mica's mouth to chase the best of his climax. So instead, he pulled back and out. His cum spurted past the tip, and he used his hand to pump his balls dry. When he was able to open his eyes again, he saw he'd coated his wife's face.

Horrified, Geoff sprang off the boy. "Shit." He grabbed the wet cloth, but Mica once more held him at bay.

With his gaze fixed on Geoff, Mica licked as much of the cum as his tongue could reach. "Love it I do," he whispered. "And...I love you."

Relief flooded Geoff, and as there was still some mess to clean up, he gently washed his wife's face again. "I'd say we are well-suited, wife. How clever of you to realize it when you saved my life." He banked the fire, then cuddled Mica to keep him warm and waited until the boy had fallen asleep before joining him, more content than he'd ever been in his life.

Epilogue

It was harder to say good-bye to his family than Mica had expected. Since his rescue, he'd come to see his father, in particular, in a new light. The man was gruff but loving in his own way. Mica had assumed the man was disappointed in having a son who wasn't a warrior. He realized that his father had never actually said anything of the kind. He'd only expected Mica to focus his efforts on serving the People instead of always looking in the distance for something better. And now, he was letting Mica go without a word of disapproval. Maybe all that had to have happened was for Mica to become a man for the two of them to find their way. Better perhaps and just as important to him, Keme and Geoff had developed a mutual respect. They spoke in low tones — about him he figured, given the way they both looked at him.

His mother was less obvious and more reserved in showing her affection. She wasn't repeating the outburst when she'd seen him come out of the cave alive, but she displayed her feelings, nevertheless, in

ways that suited her. Despite the provisions given by
the chief weighing down two pack horses, she handed
him a stuffed satchel of food so that *"hungry you must
not be"*. Then she gave a blessing, entreating the Earth
Mother to protect him and Geoff on their journey. It
was the including of his husband that brought tears to
Mica's eyes. He hugged her hard, even though he knew
she wasn't much on such physical contact.

There were tears from Alyn and Lye. The little boy
often cried when he was forced to leave Mica's arms,
but he was too young to understand how this time it
was more permanent. Mica could only hope that his
family kept his memory alive for Lye so that when they
met again — and he was determined that they would —
the child would know his big brother.

"Fear not," Alyn said as she placed Lye on her hips.
"Talk of you often we will." Her potter stood behind
her, his hand resting on her shoulder in support. After
the crisis of Lonan, his sister had had her way over
marrying someone who was not a warrior.

Geoff came over and clasped Mica's hand. "It's time
to go, darling. I want to find my men before they get
too far."

Mica understood. His husband had already given
him two more days of rest. "As you say." With a final
wave at everyone, he vaulted onto his horse and
walked it to stand beside Geoff's mount. They weren't
neck and neck, though. Geoff would always be the one
to lead, and that suited Mica just fine. He wanted
adventure, but also to be as safe as possible. He trusted
his husband to always look after him.

They left the village at a fast trot. Mica gazed around
the canyon to fix the way it looked in his memories.
He'd traveled this path many times yet had never really
paid attention to the beauty around him. The cliffs on

either side of them had always simply *been* there, nothing of note. Their formations and striations of color had served no purpose other than to help him navigate. As important as that was, it didn't negate the wonder of how they looked. He wanted to make sure that this vision of his homeland stayed in his mind. Wherever he went and whatever he saw, nothing was ever going to be as amazing as this—because it was *his* in a way nothing else would ever be, however happy he was for the rest of his life.

Geoff turned to him. "I know this must be hard, darling. I'm sorry to take you away from everyone and everything you've ever known."

Mica kicked his horse to reach out his hand to his husband. "You are my family. With you I shall always want to be."

Geoff took the proffered hand and squeezed it. "And I'm selfish enough to want you by my side." Letting go, he led them on to the mouth of the canyon. He barked out a laugh. "Well, this is a surprise."

Mica saw what he was referring to in the next instant. Geoff's men were camped just inside the canyon walls. As he and Mica approached, all the men stood. There was a stunned silence before they all cheered.

Geoff stopped in front of them and jumped off his horse. He embraced one of the men with a hearty hug and a bunch of back thumping. "Lucas, my gods! I thought you well away from here."

Lucas shrugged. "You said to make an escape if the opportunity arose, but you didn't tell me what to do if the archers hemming us in just left. They were gone without a word by the end of the second day they took you. Although I had no idea what that meant, I wasn't going to leave until I'd given you a chance to rejoin us.

I guess I had hoped you were still alive. Your timing is perfect, actually, because we were going to break camp tomorrow. Too much time had passed, and I feared you were dead after all."

Geoff put his hands on his hips and grinned. "I nearly was a few times, truth be told. Those are tales for nights around the campfire. Suffice to say, I owe my life to Mica." He gestured for him to join them.

Feeling a bit shy now that he was surrounded by his husband's men, Mica had held back. He was determined to do whatever his husband asked of him, though. And this was an easy start. He slid from his horse and went to Geoff's side, who hugged him by the waist.

Lucas looked at him with wide eyes. "The boy from the quicksand."

"My wife," Geoff corrected.

"Ah." Lucas bowed to Mica. "Lady Arbuthnott."

Mica furrowed his brows at the strange manner of address. "I am that?"

Geoff gave him a squeeze. "Yes, darling. I'm afraid so. Does it bother you?"

Mica considered it. He was the wife of a Moorcondian, so he was obligated to adopt their customs, except that's not where they were and wouldn't be for a long time. Out there in the unknown, he could be whoever he wanted.

"I prefer Mica." He hoped he wasn't being too bold, especially in front of the men his husband commanded.

Geoff gave him a quick kiss, right on the lips, in front of everyone. "Then Mica you shall be." To the others, he said, "We break camp now. There's much of the day left, and we've a long journey ahead. The People of his land have been generous with provisions, so we can move forward with more confidence." He released his hold on Mica. "I must reacquaint myself with my men and labor alongside them. Will you be all right by yourself?"

"I can help." Mica wanted to do his fair share of the work.

Geoff tapped the tip of Mica's nose with his finger. "I know you can and you will—later, once I've judged you well-rested from...everything."

Mica folded his arms and frowned. "Fine I am."

"When I say you are, darling."

Mica tapped his toe, trying to decide if he should challenge his husband on the topic of his own health. He'd resolved to let Geoff lead, but he wasn't going to follow him blindly. By the look on his face, Geoff was ready for more disagreement and would have his way.

This was not a fight Mica could win. "As you say."

Geoff gave him an approving nod. "Excellent." He leaned in so that only Mica could hear. "You must pick your battles carefully, darling. I don't expect blind obedience, but I will *never* stop doing what I think is best for you. My love allows nothing else."

Warmth spread from Mica's heart across his chest. "Fair you are not. How can I argue when you say *that* word?" He pushed the sentence out to emphasize how much he meant it."

Before Geoff left him, the small, older man came running up. "Lady Arbuthnott. Your pardon, *Mica*. I understand you will be joining us. Might I impose and pick your brain?"

"Speak more clearly, Professor Johns. My wife is mastering our mode of speech very well, but such idiomatic expressions will be difficult for him for a while still."

"My apologies again. I want to learn of your home and your culture. Was I right that you live in dwellings carved into the cliffside?"

"Yes."

"Fantastic! Come and tell me everything. I will draw what I think you are describing, and you can tell me what I get right and wrong. This is going to be so much fun," he said as he rubbed his hands together.

Mica looked at his husband. "Should I?"

"Absolutely. It will be a productive way for you to spend your time that will not worry me. Have care with my wife, Professor."

"You can count on me, Sir Geoffrey. I'm happy our adventures are to continue with you and Mica."

"As am I," Geoff agreed. "And what about you, darling? Are you ready to see the world?"

Mica stared at the horizon before him. "I am ready to see…everything."

Want to see more from this author?
Here's a taster for you to enjoy!

Treaty Brides: The Siege Bride
Samantha Cayto

Excerpt

The first slap of wind heralding the impending winter made Baron Henry Roth's eyes water. It made peering through his spyglass at the impenetrable fortress looming high above his camp even more irritating than it had already become. Nothing had changed in the weeks since he'd arrived, and he was no further along his mission of breaching the place. Every day had become the same as the last, with no end in sight.

He suppressed the desire to sigh. "Highrock is certainly well-named."

Sir Colin Beaumont, one of the few men in Moorcondia taller than Henry, leaned his elbow on Henry's shoulder. "This is what comes of you being so good at your job, Hal. The king has sent you here because he believes you are the best man to get in there and stop this rebellion. You have only yourself to blame."

Now Henry did sigh as he lowered the spyglass. "You're right, of course. But not even my prodigious mind for warfare can see a way to take that place without tremendous loss of life. I will not use the bodies of our dead men as a bridge to the gate. The siege must continue, even though it means wintering here."

"Freezing our balls off." Colin took the spyglass and looked through it himself. "How long do you think they can last up there?"

Henry had done the calculations the previous night with the information he had. "I think they can last until spring, actually...maybe longer. Cragmore has been planning this move for a long time, I'll wager, and has filled his fortress with as many provisions as that massive place can hold. Their wells ensure a plentiful supply of fresh water, so running out of food will be the only thing to bring him to heel. I don't think he's going to risk his people starving to keep this ill-gotten autonomy."

Colin snorted as he lowered the glass. "King of the North Cliffs. What nonsense. His ancestor was critical to bringing the disparate factions under the one rule of Moorcondia. This land has prospered ever since. What madness has driven him to declare autonomy, do you think?"

Henry had pondered that very question many times and still had no answer. There was rumor of the old duke losing his senses with age. That, plus the death of his older son, may have been what had tipped his mind into madness — all which was purely speculation. The old guy might simply be a greedy bastard who thought the distraction of fighting the Swarm had made Moorcondia subject to this kind of rebellion. No matter. The king wasn't going to allow Cragmore to break away into a separate country, regardless of how little strategic value the place had. Sedition was something that spread if it wasn't eradicated.

He turned to look at his camp, a sea of tents with thousands of soldiers milling about. They had the advantage militarily but for the impregnable fortress sitting high up on three sides and with sheer cliffs on the fourth one. If they could only get inside, the fight would be swift and hopefully with as little bloodshed as possible. Even if Henry weren't inclined to mercy himself, the king had made it clear — *"Bring the people of Highrock back into the fold. Don't slaughter them."*

He started threading his way through the camp to his own tent. "Tell the quartermaster we must make plans to provision us through the winter at least. I assume much of what we'll need will have to be transported to us. The locals can't supply us for much longer, and that's assuming they will continue to want to."

So far, the Cragmore residents had met his arrival with the type of indifference that came from being under someone else's control. Powerful people ruled their lives, regardless of what they thought, and as long as no one was sacking their town and homes, they went about their business, ignoring the nonsense of the ruling class — not that he could be sure no spies or saboteurs mingled among them. It was a near certainty that some of them were personally loyal to the duke.

Colin walked beside him, always a reliable bannerman and as close to a brother as a friend could be. "One thing we won't have to worry about is having enough wine."

Henry glanced up at the only other prominent building in the area. "Ah yes, the good sisters." Honoria Abbey had been in the north longer than the duke's family. The fertile land covering their hills produced excellent grapes, and the nuns living there made exquisite wine. "I assume their reverend mother has kept them apolitical."

"As far as we can tell. They are certainly quick with a smile whenever I encounter one in town."

"Hmm. I don't trust religious types overly much, as you know. We should be extra vigilant, as the only women in the world who can disarm men easily, other than whores, are nuns. A smiling woman is the greatest weapon to use against a man."

"We are terribly dumb creatures," Colin agreed.

"Ruled by our cocks and stomachs and made vulnerable by our inflated confidence. If we have to remain in this soon-to-be frozen field of mud, we must be careful not to give the duke any information that can strengthen his position. He has the strategic advantage of his location, but we have time on our hands."

"And idleness is the worst enemy for soldiers. I'll remain vigilant. Never fear, Hal."

Henry clapped his friend's back. "I have no doubt, and if we must linger in this place, we at least have each other for company." He didn't elaborate, because Colin understood. Throughout long campaigns, they would spend hours talking and playing chess and also giving each other pleasure. It was a casual thing between them, especially as Colin planned on marrying and fathering children at some point when he was ready to give up soldiering, while Henry had no such interest. He just liked having his needs tended to on a regular basis and disliked using whorehouses. The boys there were often under the duress of having no other options in life, and Henry didn't like preying on others — and neither did his friend. A quick hand or blow job with Colin was the best solution. It was a way of relieving stress without worrying about pressuring those under their command.

Colin cleared his throat. "All this talk of wine has made me thirsty. Shall we retire to your tent for a cup or two?"

Henry was about to agree when a woman's strident voice caught his attention. He turned his head toward the edge of the camp where a road out of town was located. "What's that?" He changed course to investigate.

The guards tasked with guarding who came in and out of town were clustered around a wagon filled with casks. Three nuns stood to one side while a fourth one was giving the sergeant the cutting edge of her tongue.

"You have no right to impede our journey. We have a delivery to make."

The older man, well-used to dealing with difficult encounters of this kind, was clearly trying to keep his temper. "Holy sister, my job is to keep the people of the north here, where they belong. We can't have the enemies of the king wandering about the country, now can we?"

The woman lifted her chin, her green wimple fluttering in the wind. "My good man, surely you aren't suggesting that we sisters are soldiers or spies? We make wine and this," she added with a wave at the wagon, "is an order for our customer in the valley. We only ask to deliver it. I assure you we will return to our abbey within a few days. And," she added with a very un-nun-like sneer, "we shall *not* be slitting your throats while you sleep when we do so."

The guard tried for affable. "Of course not, madam. But a simple solution is to sell your casks to us. We are happy to buy them from you, and our coin is as good as anyone else's."

"Oh, so now you demand that we renege on our order to a long-standing customer? You'll buy our wine

I'm sure for so long as you're here. By the time you're gone, the people outside of the north will have found other suppliers. Is your remit from the king to destroy the abbey's economy?"

This situation had taken a dark turn. Henry hurried to intervene. "What is all this?"

His arrival obviously relieved the guard. He tipped his helmet. "My lord."

The nun turned her gaze on him, her eyes brimming with fury. "You are Baron Roth?"

Henry sketched a bow. "I am."

"Then tell your men to let us pass. We merely mean to go about our business, regardless of your ridiculous dispute with the duke. It has nothing to do with us. My sisters and I are harmless."

Henry doubted that was entirely true. He had a feeling that this nun would stick a knife in one's belly if provoked. The other three were meeker, their heads bowed and hands clasped in front of them. There was very little visible, as was always the case with nuns, being dressed as they were with wimples, long robes and loose belts. They appeared younger than their spokeswoman. The one in the middle in particular had creamy skin that looked as if it didn't get much sun. Now, that was interesting. The others' faces were more golden, as were their hands. Their necks were covered tightly, and while two of them sported slender columns that led into their habits, the middle one's throat looked a little thicker.

Henry trusted his gut. It had saved his life on occasion. At the moment, it was telling him that something was wrong. He approached the three nuns and peered at them more closely. The slight stiffening in all four women told him he was on to something. He ran his gaze down the middle nun, noting her larger hands and how the boots peeking out from the hem of the habit were of excellent quality compared to the others. As he reached the nun and stared hard at her, the woman lifted her face and peered back at him with vivid blue eyes. There was some trepidation in that gaze, but also defiance and the kind of haughtiness that was bred into nobility.

Knowing he took a risk that would only enrage the local population, Henry listened to his gut and yanked the wimple off the nun's head. A cascade of silky blond hair, so pale it was nearly white, tumbled out and the Adam's apple he'd been sure lay behind the cloth was exposed.

Henry was struck dumb for a moment, the boy's beauty that arresting. When he'd recovered his wits, he let a slow smile spread across his face. "Well, well, who do we have here?"

Kellen of Cragmore tightened his grip to keep the trembling from showing. He'd known this idea had been a foolish risk. He should have stayed hidden in the abbey instead of letting the Reverend Mother talk him into this mad scheme to spirit him away to his mother's people in the south. And he would have resisted more if he hadn't also been afraid that the king's men would somehow discover him and punish the nuns for harboring the son of a traitor who had picked a fight he couldn't possibly win. Now, the good women, who had been nothing but kind to him, were in trouble anyway.

He lifted his chin and glared with more bravado than he felt into the dark eyes of the fearsome Baron Roth. The man had a reputation of being a consummate soldier, and seeing him up close with his short black hair, square jaw and towering height, he could believe everything he'd ever heard about the man. But his reputation included being fair. Kellen could reason with him. He had to.

"I am Kellen of Cragmore."

Roth raised one eyebrow. "The duke's surviving son. How intriguing. What are you doing dressed as a nun and sneaking past my siege?"

Kellen licked his lips, trying to marshal his answer. He didn't miss the way the baron's gaze tracked his movements. And the look in his eyes—hungry—was something he was used to seeing, too. Usually that kind of interest from a powerful man made him afraid. Somehow that wasn't happening this time. If anything, he felt…intrigued. And if he were bold enough, that kind of lust could be used against a man. The trouble was, Kellen had never been daring in his life.

"I was at the abbey when you arrived. They were only trying to keep me safe." He stiffened his spine and gave the baron as fierce a look as he could manage, given that he barely reached the man's chest. "You will not punish them for this. They have nothing to do with my father's plans and acted only out of concern for me."

Roth's expression turned thoughtful. "What were you doing at the abbey?"

Before Kellen could answer, Sister Winnifred stepped toward them. "Leave him be. Kellen is a good boy, only interested in winemaking. He spends most of his days with us, has nothing to do with his father's perfidy and is no danger to you."

"I'm not so sure about that," the baron murmured, his intense gaze making Kellen shake again. 'His presence is…disturbing." Then the man smiled at him.

Kellen nearly took a step back from the scrutiny, except there was nowhere to go, and one thing he'd learned in life about powerful men was to never let them see your fear. "I am of no consequence. With my brother's death, my sister has become my father's heir. She sits up there with him," he added with a jut of his chin in the direction of Highrock. "I'm not part of their effort to leave Moorcondia. I doubt they've even noticed I'm not in the castle." That was sadly true. He was so unlike the rest of his family that they'd ceased to pay any attention to him.

A terrifying thought occurred to him. "They won't surrender to save me, either. I can't be used to your advantage."

The baron chuckled as he shook his head, the low timber of his voice skittering along Kellen's skin. "I'm not going to strap you to a catapult and threaten to send you over the wall if they don't open the gates. That doesn't mean, however, that you don't have your uses. I can think of a few already." His tone implied something that was menacing on a level that had nothing to do with warfare.

The baron turned on his heels to face Sister Winnifred. "You may continue on your way, madam. But I hope you will also sell us your most excellent wine. It's going to be a long winter."

The nun's lips thinned. "By the grace of the gods, we serve all people as best we can. You will have your wine, my lord, like any good customer. But you will hand the boy back to us, as well. We'll make sure he stays in the abbey and out of your way."

Kellen had to blink back sudden tears at how this woman was defying a dangerous man on his behalf, even as he knew she wasn't going to get her way. "It's all right, sister. You've all been very kind to me, but I must go with the baron. My birthright ensures that I become a political prisoner. There's nothing either of us can do about that, and I want you all to be safe. It will give me peace of mind. Please."

Before the woman could respond, Roth intervened. "Madam, I give you my word that I won't harm a hair on his beautiful head. I simply can't let him go, though. However he feels about his father's actions, as the man's son, he can become a person for sympathizers to rally around, whether he wants to be or not. He's actually safer with me than he would be out in the world."

Kellen knew the baron was right, although as far as Kellen was concerned, there was no safe place for him. The moment his father and sister had openly rebelled against the king, they'd sealed his fate. He would never be free again...not really. He shot Winnifred an imploring look.

The nun gave a curt nod. "I shall do as asked, because I obviously have no choice. May the gods be with you, Kellen." She smiled at him before glaring at the baron. "And may the gods shrivel your manhood if you break your word."

Roth held out his hands. "I assure you, madam, I want no trouble from your good self or the gods. Safe travels." Then he took Kellen by the elbow, his touch firm, yet not painful. "Let's go to my tent and have a little talk, shall we?"

Kellen had no choice but to stumble along, trying to match the man's long strides. With them came a knight who was even taller than the baron, although not as broad or thickly muscled. As they made their way, soldiers gaped at him openly. They didn't jeer at him, a mark of respect, he thought, for their commander. In fact, the looks on the men's faces were that of respect and even affection—if one could ascribe such a sentiment to hardened fighters. Roth was in full command of his men, obviously, and that allayed Kellen's fear that the siege would cause great trouble in town from bored men spoiling for a fight.

It was no surprise when they entered the biggest tent in the camp. Inside was a luxurious place that made even Highrock look shabby. War he might be fighting, but the baron was going to spend the siege walking on plush carpets and sleeping in a large bed sitting on a platform. There was a desk and a few chairs, a low table and tall cupboards for clothing. The baron was dressed plainly in all black, with leather pants that hugged his thick thighs, shiny boots up to his knees and a tunic straining from his broad chest. His belt held a big scabbard with a long sword sporting a simple hilt. No jewels flashed on it the way his brother's had.

The man led Kellen to a chair by a fire pit located under an opening to let smoke out. It wasn't lit, not yet, but it would be soon, given the harsh winter that was coming. "Make yourself comfortable, my lord."

Kellen had no choice, and besides, he was happy to give his shaky knees a rest. He pulled the wimple completely off and ran his fingers through his hair. He watched the men as they spoke with one another.

"Shall I secure a tent to hold our guest, Hal?"

Kellen blinked at the familiar address, then studied the way the men stood close to each other and at their expressions. *They are lovers.* For some reason, the thought disappointed him. *Don't be ridiculous.*

Roth gave him the side-eyes. "That won't be necessary, Colin, but see if my page can rustle up more suitable clothes for the boy. As fetching as he is in even a simple nun's habit, I'd see him dressed in a manner suitable for his station."

"As you say, my lord." Before the knight left, he winked at Kellen. "Our time here has just gotten more interesting — for one of us, anyway."

Kellen was still trying to decipher what the man meant by that when the baron came over and threw himself into the nearby chair. He stretched his impossibly long legs out and clasped his hands on his lap — the perfect picture of a man at ease. "So, Lord Kellen, you like making wine, do you?"

Kellen wanted to refuse to answer, but that wouldn't accomplish anything, and he didn't want to aggravate the man for fear he might take it out on the nuns after all. "I do."

"Why?"

Now he was confused. He'd expected to be peppered with questions about the strategic strengths of his father's castle. This line of questioning befuddled him. Perhaps the baron wasn't as smart a soldier as his reputation implied.

Kellen shrugged. "It's interesting, that's all. The soil here grows wonderful grapes that with patience and effort produces a wine that is full-bodied and fruity without being overly sweet. It keeps me occupied, in any event. Highrock will never be mine, and I have no aptitude for soldiering."

"No indeed, you are too delicate for battle — at least the kind waged by soldiers."

Kellen frowned at that cryptic remark, although the heated gaze the baron sent his way made his cheeks hot. He looked elsewhere to break the connection. "What do you intend to do with me if you aren't going to lock me up in another tent?" The idea that he might be put on display in a cage in the open drained the blood from his face.

"Oh that's an easy question to answer. You're going to stay here…with me."

Kellen whipped his head around. "What? Your tent is big, baron, I'll grant you that, but it hardly contains space for two to occupy while giving each other room. And you must confer with your men in here. Surely you don't want me to privy to your strategies." His heartbeat ticked up, although whether it was from fear or something else — something entirely inappropriate — he didn't know.

The baron crossed his ankles and slouched even more in his chair. "I'm not worried about any of that, my lord. You'll never be able to help your father with whatever you hear, if for no other reason than he's not letting anyone in. Not even for his own son would he risk lowering his drawbridge. We're stuck with each other for the remainder of this siege, I'm afraid." He waved his hand. "Well, I'm not disappointed about that."

To quell his renewed shaking, Kellen crossed his arms. "You'll get nothing useful out of me. I'll be a pointless irritant for so long as you keep me prisoner in here, underfoot at every turn. You'll probably trip over me when you get up in the morning, because I tend to sprawl when I sleep." He hadn't meant to raise such an intimate subject as his sleeping habits, but the words were out and there was no taking them back.

The baron's response sent a chill up his spine.

Roth threw his head back and laughed, then said, "My dear Lord Kellen, I'm not worried about tripping over you because you won't be sleeping on the floor. You'll be sharing my bed."

About the Author

Samantha Cayto is a Boston-area native who practices as a business lawyer by day while writing erotic romance at night—the steamier the better. She likes to push the envelope when it comes to writing about passion and is delighted other women agree that guy-on-guy sex is the hottest ever.

She lives a typical suburban life with her husband, three kids and four dogs. Her children don't understand why they can't read what she writes, but her husband is always willing to lend her a hand—and anything else—when she needs to choreograph a scene.

Samantha loves to hear from readers. You can find her contact information, website details and author profile page at https://www.firstforromance.com/

PUBLISHING

Sign up for our newsletter and find out about all our romance book releases, eBook sales and promotions, sneak peeks and FREE romance books!